THE TROUBLE LEGACY

E.R. FALLON
KJ FALLON

www.bloodhoundbooks.com

Print ISBN978-1-914614-19-4

ALSO BY E.R. FALLON

PROLOGUE

W ho I am is not important. The story I have to tell you is. After the incident, Camille O'Brien was out of commission for a few months while she recuperated from being shot in the chest by Violet McCarthy. As for Violet, she wasn't unscathed, and suffered a gunshot wound to the neck inflicted by Camille, but had been sent home relatively early considering. Violet relished in the fact that she'd returned home while Camille, she hoped, was still suffering in the hospital.

In the end, Camille had the last laugh, as at that time, Violet was still being watched by the police, especially by Detective Seale. Camille's mother, Sheila, ran the neighborhood and worked under the Italian mob with the help of Camille's boyfriend, Johnny Garcia Jr., and with Violet's mother, Catherine, serving a prison sentence for murder and racketeering, Violet was under a lot of pressure and forced to make an agreement with them. The agreement allowed her to control her section of the neighborhood, if she kept her hands off everything else. But it gave her a chance to rebuild her family's pub, *McBurney's*, which had been destroyed by arson.

Neither Camille nor Violet nor their families and associates went to the police after the shootout. There were private doctors who helped gangsters with their injuries, so even the hospital didn't know what had happened.

Eventually, Camille left the hospital, although with nerve damage on the left side of her body, which would require her to use a cane for the rest of her life. True, she rather liked the elegant choice she had made—an expensive black walking stick hand-made in Italy, with a sterling silver handle. If it was going to be a permanent and needed accessory, it was going to make a statement. Johnny became her permanent chauffer and did so lovingly. Around 1986, they married. After the death of Johnny's first wife in 1987, she adopted Johnny's daughter from that marriage, Phoebe, and, over time, Camille became like a second mother to the girl.

But some things never changed. They never went away. The past was always there.

1

What separated Thomas 'Tommy' Carmine from the other cops in his division was the fact that his grandfather, Sean McCarthy, had been an Irish gangster. Tommy himself was very much aware about who his grandfather was, which was why he'd taken his father's last name after his father's death years ago. Of course, Tommy's father also had been a gangster, an Italian one. But in the area of New York where Tommy worked as a policeman, the McCarthy name was synonymous with crime, the Carmine name less so.

Tommy hadn't always wanted to be a policeman, but after his father's murder, he started thinking about it. His mother, Violet, had seemed surprised when he'd told her about his decision, but she gave him her congratulations. His mother had also been in trouble with the law a few times, but after her injury years ago that all seemed to be behind her. She now spent her days running their family's pub, with the help of her live-in boyfriend, Sam.

Tommy didn't talk about who his family was with most people outside the neighborhood where he grew up, including his boss, his lieutenant.

One day, Lieutenant Andrews asked Tommy to come into his office. The request took Tommy by surprise, as he wasn't expecting it, and the lieutenant mostly didn't deal with ordinary police officers like Tommy. Lieutenant Andrews mostly dealt with detectives, which Tommy wanted to be, and he wouldn't let anything interfere with that.

Tommy rose from his desk, filled with nerves, and knocked on Andrews' door though it was opened.

"It's Officer Carmine, sir," he said.

"Come in," the lieutenant said in his baritone.

Tommy straightened his uniform then entered the office. "Do you want me to close the door, sir?" he asked Andrews.

"Yeah, go ahead."

Tommy shut the door and stood in front of the lieutenant's wide, gleaming wood desk. "You asked to see me, sir?"

"Yeah, there's something I need to discuss with you," Andrews said, finally looking up at Tommy from the papers on his desk.

Tommy swallowed. "Yes, sir?"

"Sit down, Officer Carmine," he said, and so Tommy did.

He sat in silence, waiting for Andrews to elaborate, but his one hand gripped the edge of the chair in anticipation.

"The neighborhood where you grew up, do you still have connections there? The higher-ups mentioned to me that you said you were from there."

Tommy thought that this was it. They'd found out he was a McCarthy. He sat up straighter and readied to defend himself. "I can explain," he started to say.

"I need your help," Andrews said.

Tommy's posture relaxed a little, although it was clear to him that Andrews still didn't know he was a McCarthy. "With what, sir?" he asked.

"I heard you want to be a detective."

"Yes, that's true. I do."

"Good." He paused. "There's been some bad goings-on in the neighborhood where I heard you grew up."

"What kind of on-goings?" Tommy asked, though silently he prayed that his mother wasn't up to her old tricks.

"There's a heroin ring that every narcotics guy in the city wants to take down," Andrews said, looking at him. "You're one of the few cops in this city from that neighborhood."

"I don't live there anymore," Tommy said, quickly. He lived just outside of it. Investigating the neighborhood would mean investigating its people which could mean betraying those he knew. Everyone in the old neighborhood still viewed him as 'one of them', even though he was a cop, but once he started nosing around and asking them questions, that would change.

"Doesn't matter where you're from now. You were from there, and that's just what we need: someone familiar with the area. Another station is in charge of the investigation, but they put out a call for a local, and we had one, you."

Tommy hesitated, but internally, he knew that this was a quest he couldn't refuse. "Of course, sir. When do I start?"

"Very soon. We'll have another one of the officers finish up any outstanding paperwork for other cases. And there's something in this for you, Officer Carmine." He smiled as though he would reveal something that would pleasantly surprise Tommy.

A raise? Tommy thought.

"You want to be a detective, isn't that right?"

"Yes, sir, I do."

"Then you work this case, and we'll promote you to detective."

Tommy filled with excitement and tension. Excitement, because this was his dream, and tension because he didn't know how he would keep his friends and family out of it. But he would think of something. He always did.

"You won't be working alone, of course," Andrews said. "You'll be working alongside a detective, a woman, from the other station. I think her last name is Fitzpatrick. I'm not sure of her first name."

"Detective Fitzpatrick," Tommy said. "I'm not sure I've ever met her before."

"You probably haven't, but I'm sure you'll get along. I've heard good things about her. I'll set up a meeting with the both of you soon."

"Yes, sir," Tommy said.

"You can go now," Andrews said, and waved him off.

Tommy left the office, feeling proud and apprehensive at the same time. After all, being a detective was what he wanted, but he didn't expect to have to return to the old neighborhood to do so, and he didn't expect to have to spy on those he cared about. Tommy, loyal to a fault, questioned if he'd be able to do the job, and if he couldn't, how would we explain that to Lieutenant Andrews?

The incident with Camille O'Brien hadn't changed Violet McCarthy much. It hadn't put Violet in her place, although she pretended to everyone that it had, especially to Camille and her husband, Johnny Garcia, who now ran the neighborhood rackets together, along with help from Camille's mother, Sheila. She and Camille had developed a silent understanding and mostly stayed out of each other's way. But deep down inside Violet still very much longed for the old days of the McCarthys having full control over the neighborhood.

Violet's boyfriend, the tall, handsome, and fair-haired Sam

Paul, appeared from out of the storage area of the pub. It was early morning and there was always much work to be done before the pub opened. Violet watched him from where she stood behind the bar. The odds had been against them over the years, but they had ended up staying together after a brief breakup. Sam had come to work with Violet at the pub after he lost his job in banking. He had backed a loan for Violet to rebuild the tavern after the arson attack. Then she defaulted on it. She had given Sam's bank an income statement that made it look like she made more money than she actually had, and Sam was aware of that. He spent some time in prison as a result, where he had been the victim of a violent assault. Violet knew he didn't like to discuss what happened but she did know that it troubled him greatly.

Sam went to the bar and smiled at Violet. "Have I told you how happy I am to be with you?"

Violet laughed slightly. "Yes, many times," she said with a smile.

"Well, I'm going to say it again, because I can't stop saying it. I love you, Violet." He rested his hand on the top of the bar and Violet tried not to stare at the way it tremored, which it had done once in a while ever since his assault, because she knew it made him self-conscious.

Violet poured them each a cup of coffee and they began to chat about other things. "When's the next shipment coming in?" she asked Sam.

"The boat's supposed to dock today. Or so the Swede said."

The Swede was the name of their heroin supplier, and after getting it from him, Violet and Sam then had their guys distribute it around the city. The whole thing made Violet feel slightly conflicted. After all, the McCarthys' criminal enterprise dated back to Violet's grandfather, Sean McCarthy, who thought drug dealers were the 'scum of the earth' and refused to partake in it.

But Violet reasoned times had changed and it was a different era, and she and Sam had to do what they needed to in order to survive. After her bar had burned down and Camille O'Brien took everything, Violet had been on the dole for a while so that she could raise her son alone. With her mother in prison, it was just her and Tommy. Then Sam came back into their lives. It had been difficult raising Tommy without her mother's help, but she'd eventually got back together with Sam and he became her rock. The heroin business had given both of them a fresh start.

They had managed to keep Camille, who now went by the name Camille Garcia after her marriage to Johnny, out of their business, for now, but the bigger things became and the less small time they were, the more Violet worried Camille would want a piece of the action. But Violet and Sam were being smart about it. They weren't being obvious, and were saving their money instead of spending it on things like new cars. But someday, they planned to sell the pub and start a new life in warm, sunny Florida. Sam had been worried that Violet would start using again when they began dealing, and she'd certainly been tempted to. But so far, she hadn't.

The pub wasn't opened for the day yet, but there was a knock on the front door and both looked to see who it was. Violet's son, Tommy, stood outside waving at them.

Violet left the bar to open the door, nearly running, for she hadn't seen her beloved son in weeks.

"Tommy," she said, embracing him as soon as the door opened.

"How are you, Ma?" her handsome son asked, looking down at her. Tommy had the same dark good looks as his Italian father and had Violet's father's great height.

"Oh, you know, the same. It's been two weeks since I last saw you," Violet said with a smile, delighted to see her boy again.

"You need to visit your mother more often," she said, scolding him in jest.

"Sorry about that," Tommy said. He wasn't a mama's boy, but Violet knew she had a slight hold over him.

Violet waited for him to acknowledge Sam, whom Tommy had always had a tense relationship with. He'd never replace Tommy's father, who had died in a gangland shootout years ago when Tommy was just a boy, but Sam tried his best to be there for Tommy even if he resisted his affection.

Tommy waved at Sam, who said hello, but didn't speak to him. Violet sighed. These were her two favorite men in the world, and she wanted them to get along, but no matter how hard she tried, some things couldn't be fixed.

Sam sat down at the bar and lit a cigarette, a habit he'd acquired in prison, and smoked in silence as Violet and Tommy chatted. He had learned to keep his distance when Tommy was there.

"How have you been?" Violet asked her son. "What's new? You found a girlfriend yet?" Violet was always teasing him about his never-ending variety of women.

"There's no one special."

"Of course not," Violet quipped. "You never stay with them long enough to get to know them. When am I gonna get a grandchild?"

Tommy blushed. "Maybe someday, Ma. I just haven't found the right girl. So, how's business?" he asked. Violet thought to change the subject. He meant the pub, of course, not the heroin business, of which he knew nothing about.

"Good," Violet said. "We're doing well here." Actually, with the heroin operation as their main racket in the neighborhood, they were doing very well. Which was why Violet needed to keep it out of Camille's clutches.

"I have some good news," Tommy said. "I'm up for a promotion at work."

With the main business in her family heritage being crime, Violet didn't love that her son had become a police officer, but Tommy seemed to genuinely like what he did for a living, and because Violet loved her son, she was happy for him. "If I do good, they'll make me a detective."

"That's great, Tommy," she said. Violet reasoned Tommy had become a cop because his father was a gangster, and with his grandmother also in prison, Violet figured her son felt like he had to make amends. Violet's mother Catherine had been beloved to Tommy when he was a boy, but they didn't discuss her much these days, as whenever Violet brought her up, Tommy became upset. At least Catherine had become sober while in prison, as they had a special program, and she knew Tommy was proud of his grandmother for that.

"I'm proud of you," Violet said, and stood on her toes to kiss her son on the cheek. She knew that Tommy dreamed of being a detective.

"Thanks," Tommy replied. "It's not going to be easy though. I have to bring in a certain collar."

"Who do you have to arrest?" she asked him, because sometimes Tommy dropped hints about the criminal on-goings in the neighborhood, and as a cop, he knew things even she didn't know.

"You know I can't tell you that, ma," Tommy said with a smile. He followed the rules by the book.

"Can't you give me even a little hint?" Violet teased her son, but she really wanted to know.

"No, I can't tell you," Tommy said with a slight smile.

"Tommy, please! Tell me."

Tommy sighed. "Supposedly there's a heroin ring in your neighborhood, and I'm going to help bring them down."

"In this neighborhood?" Violet said quietly, feigning shock, but her knees almost buckled. Tommy knew that his great-grandfather and father had been gangsters, and his grandmother had done something unscrupulous to end up in jail, but he thought that Violet had left all of that behind her and now just owned a pub with her boyfriend. If what Tommy was saying held weight, then that meant that Tommy was after her.

"Yeah," Tommy said. "Right here in this neighborhood. Can you believe it? It's crazy."

Violet stood there in silence, thinking about the ring being run out of the secret room they'd built downstairs during the rebuild after the fire. "No, I can't believe it," she finally said, trying to act surprised. "That's really frightening."

"So, you haven't heard anything about it?" Tommy asked her. "I know that sometimes people who come to the bar talk."

Violet contemplated what to say. "I haven't heard anything, Tommy," she said after a moment. "But I can tell you that if there's trouble in the neighborhood, then there's almost certainly one person to blame."

"You are going to say Camille O'Brien?" Tommy asked. "I know how much you dislike her."

"I just don't care for her. She's trouble," Violet said with a wave of her hand.

Camille might have no longer lived in the neighborhood, but she still controlled it afar, from her suburban palace, while Violet was stuck living with Sam above the pub.

"Every cop in the neighborhood knows her family's reputation, but there's never anything about drugs connected to her," Tommy said.

"That's not what I hear," Violet lied.

"Do you know something, Ma?" Tommy said when she didn't elaborate.

Violet didn't like lying to her son, but she needed him to stay clear of her and Sam's operation, for the sake of their relationship.

"All I'm saying is, she's bad news, and if anyone's dabbling in smack in this neighborhood, it'd be her."

"Thanks, Ma. I'll look into it," Tommy said, but he sounded doubtful, and Violet was unsure how to convince him, he was so stubborn.

2

To say that Camille O'Brien disliked Violet McCarthy would have been an understatement. She hated that bitch with everything she had, and her hatred ran deep in her veins. It was because of Violet that Camille had to mostly use a cane.

Her mother Sheila had remarried years ago, to a retired mob lawyer, and around that same time she had reluctantly handed control of the neighborhood racket back to Camille and Johnny after Camille recovered from her injury. Through her step-father, Camille got a stepbrother, Mickey, also a criminal lawyer, in her step-father's former firm.

She and Johnny lived in the suburbs now, but still ran their old neighborhood in the city, where they kept an apartment, and kept watch over everything. They were very much known through the various thugs they employed to be their eyes and ears. The people in the neighborhood very much feared them.

Camille didn't see much of Violet McCarthy these days, but she knew that Violet still lived in the old neighborhood and still ran her family's pub. Camille had her men keep a special eye on Violet because she sure as hell didn't trust her not to try to regain control over the neighborhood rackets that involved illegal gambling, loan sharking and a few other unsavory dealings. But they weren't perfect, and sometimes they missed things.

In the morning, Camille stirred in bed when she heard someone pulling into the driveway of her house. She nudged Johnny awake next to her.

"What's going on, baby?" he asked sleepily. "You want to make love?" He grinned.

Camille shushed him. They weren't expecting any visitors, not at that early hour, and it wasn't Phoebe coming home after a night out. Camille's stepdaughter was only in high school, and they kept a strict eye on her.

"Someone's outside," Camille said, waiting for them to knock on the door.

"We aren't expecting anybody. So who the hell is it?" Johnny said.

"Exactly."

Johnny started to rise. "I'll go see who the hell it is."

Camille touched his arm. "I'll go with you."

"No, you're the woman, you stay," Johnny said with a smile, as if teasing her. He reached for his gun on the dresser.

Camille smiled back. "We do everything together," she reminded him.

"All right," Johnny grinned. "We'll go together."

Camille put on her own bathrobe. Just because she used a cane didn't mean she needed help all the time, and she sure as hell wasn't going to ask anyone for it. But Johnny knew to offer her help when she really needed it, and so he put her slippers on for her.

They left their bedroom and checked on Phoebe, who was snoring lightly in her bedroom. The knock came from outside, and they walked downstairs quietly together, with Johnny assisting Camille down the steps.

Was it the police? Johnny kept his gun drawn when he shouted, "Who is it?" through the door. A lot of people wanted them dead, people such as cops and other gangsters.

"Hey, Johnny, it's Anton," the familiar voice said.

"What the fuck?" Johnny replied.

Camille stepped out from behind him to open the door. Anton worked for Mrs. Valeria and her husband, a Russian gangster who'd recently been released from prison. Camille and Johnny had made a pact with the Russians long ago and they still did business with them. They trusted Anton.

"Jesus, Anton, you scared the shit out of us," Camille told him.

"Sorry about that," Anton said in his heavy accent. "Guess I should've called ahead. I forgot to." He smiled sheepishly.

Johnny invited him inside and shut the door.

"I know it's early," Anton said.

"Yeah, Phoebe's sleeping," Camille replied.

"Want some coffee?" Johnny asked their guest.

"Yeah, I'd love some."

They walked into the sun-filled kitchen and Johnny prepared the coffee while Camille and Anton sat at the table.

"Okay, I'll keep it short," Anton told them. "Mrs. Valeria wanted me to personally invite the both of you to her birthday party. It's the first big one she's had since her old man was released from jail."

This wasn't an invitation they could think about, so both eagerly agreed to attend. They started to drink the coffee and Anton said, "I saw Tommy the other day, Violet's son."

"I know who he is," Camille said. They trusted Anton, but both knew he had a soft spot for Tommy, from dating the guy's mother years ago.

"Tommy mentioned that he's looking to bust a huge heroin

ring in your neighborhood," Anton said carefully. He knew Camille had a temper.

She and Johnny knew Violet was selling some drugs, but it was so small time they didn't give a shit about it. Hell, it was practically nothing. So who the fuck was dealing big time in her neighborhood?

"Wait a second," Camille said, her face heated from rage. "It's Violet. That bitch has grown her operation."

"Yeah, looks that way," Anton said quietly. "Of course, Tommy doesn't know it's his mother who's behind it."

"Who's giving her the goods?" Johnny asked.

"We aren't supplying her," Anton reassured both. "I heard it's this new guy. They call him the Swede because he's from there. I don't think Tommy knows this yet."

Camille used to worry that moving out of the city neighborhood and into the suburbs would mean they couldn't keep a proper eye on things, and now her fear had come true. Although she and Johnny had never had children of their own — the doctors had told her she couldn't—she had become like a mother to Phoebe over the years, and perhaps it had softened her heart. Perhaps a little too much.

Camille and Johnny looked at each other, and each knew what the other was thinking: Violet was becoming too powerful, and there was no fucking way they were going to let her control the neighborhood like she had years ago, before they'd won control. They'd get what Violet apparently now had, no matter what it took.

With Johnny and Phoebe, Camille acted like a normal wife and mother, and so she prepared dinner for her family that night. Afterwards, Phoebe went to see a movie with her friends and

Camille sat with Johnny in the living room, watching television. Suddenly, Johnny got up and went to the window and pulled back the curtain.

"What's wrong?" Camille asked him over the sounds of the TV show. "Phoebe won't be back for a while."

"I noticed a car parked outside earlier, and I want to make sure it isn't still there. Someone was sitting inside it. I got a bad feeling about it."

"You think the cops are watching us?" Camille asked.

"Not sure," Johnny said. "The fucker's still there," he sounded exasperated.

"What are you going to do? You can't kill them just for parking outside. Come, sit down, watch TV."

"I don't like the looks of it," Johnny said, dropping the curtain. "Like I said, I got a bad feeling."

Camille sighed, annoyed. She thought he was overreacting and wanted to resume watching TV.

"Is it a man or a woman?" she asked to appease him.

"I think it's a guy."

"You think it's him again, don't you?" Camille said, because this wasn't the first time this had happened.

"Yeah, I do."

Him. Billy. The only other man she'd ever loved besides Johnny, and the man she'd almost married. They'd broken up, but Billy had pursued her again years ago as she recovered from her injury, but she'd stuck with Johnny. Not long after that, Billy was kicked out of the Italian mob for being a heroin addict. Camille hadn't known about Billy's addiction, but when she'd heard the news she'd been devastated for him. She hadn't been in touch with him for years. The last she had heard of him, he was living with a prostitute named Pillow.

"We don't know it's him," Camille told Johnny. "We've never seen them; it could be anyone."

"Who the hell else would be stalking you? That guy was fucking obsessed with you, remember?"

Camille remembered, all right. The only other person who had loved her as intensely as Billy was Johnny.

Camille waved him off. "That was such a long time ago. He's probably forgotten about me."

"But you haven't forgotten about him," Johnny remarked. "You met him when you were both teenagers, how could you ever forget your first love?"

"I don't have feelings for him anymore, but I do feel sorry for him."

"I've had enough," Johnny said, storming out of the house without his gun, but with his fists ready.

"Stop," Camille said, rising from the couch. "You don't even know it's him—" Her voice broke, because as much as she loved Johnny, she *did* still have feelings for her first love, Billy.

But it was too late. The front door flew open and Johnny was outside, running down the steps, ready to pummel the shit out of Billy or whoever was in the nearby car. Camille rushed after him as he ran the length of the sidewalk and chased after the car, an older model, as it sped away.

"Johnny, leave it be," she told him, rubbing his back as he panted. "You're too old to be doing this, you're gonna get yourself killed."

"If I'd brought my gun out with me, then I could've shot the bastard's tires and he wouldn't have got away. I shouldn't have let him get away like that. Now he's gonna keep on coming back, bothering us."

"If you'd done that, then the cops would show up and we don't need that right now. Remember, in this neighborhood people think we're good people, not like how they view us in the city. Anyway, I'm not sure it is a guy," Camille stated.

"If it's not Billy, then who is it?" Johnny asked.

"I'm not sure," Camille answered honestly, suddenly very concerned. "In the meantime, we should have some of the guys watch our house. Just one car, though. The neighbors won't like it if there are more."

They lived in what you would call a "respectable" suburban neighborhood, a far cry from the urban tenements of their childhoods, and the men who worked for them weren't what you would call respectable types. They very much looked like the mean thugs they were.

"You're frightened," Johnny said, noticing her trembling. "I don't like anyone scaring you." He touched her arm to comfort her.

"I'll be fine," Camille said, unwilling to let her guard down even in front of the man she loved. "Come on, let's go back inside," she said, holding his hand.

Narcotics detective Dana Fitzpatrick sat across from her informant in the crowded diner. She had just moved to New York City from across the river, and had only recently settled into her new job. The informant, a tall, hulking young man named Joseph, looked directly at her and lied. Dana knew he was frightened, as most men in his shoes would be. He had agreed to snitch in order to not be sent to prison. But now he was having second thoughts.

"I think you know who could be behind it," she said to him, about the neighborhood heroin ring she was trying to bust. "You don't have to be afraid."

"You don't know these people like I do," he said, shaking his head, his voice trembling.

Dana knew how scared he must have really been, for the voice of such a big man to tremble this way. She struggled to breathe amongst the smoke from the customers' cigarettes. A city-wide ban on smoking indoors was merely a week away.

"We can protect you," she offered. Then when he still hesitated, she said, "We've already done a lot for you. You owe us."

"I've told you everything I know. I don't know their names."

"I don't believe you," Dana replied. "If you're so frightened of them, then you must know their names."

"I don't get nothing in return for helping you this time. I'm already out of jail."

Dana made a fist and slammed it on the table. A couple of people stared in their direction for a moment, but quickly looked away. If Joseph wanted to be difficult, then she would let him know her displeasure. Dana knew that while Joseph was a big, strong guy, anger, even from a woman, unsettled him.

He leaned away from the table. "How much do you want to know?" he asked her quietly.

"I need a name and a location, if you have one."

"You're new to the area, right?" Joseph asked her.

Dana nodded slowly, wondering what he was about to ask her.

"So, you don't know the history of this neighborhood."

"I know some of it."

"But not everything."

"You see, my sources tell me that the McCarthys are back," Joseph said.

"The McCarthys?"

"Yeah, Violet McCarthy. She and her mother used to run things in this neighborhood, before her mother got sent to jail."

"I thought that Johnny Garcia and his wife, Camille, ran things, and everyone knows that drugs are not a part of their operation, at least, not currently."

"Now they do, but going years back, it was Violet and her

20

mother who ran things. And before that, Violet's grandfather was the boss. Her grandfather didn't deal with drugs, but Violet's different. She's willing to try anything. That's the word on the street."

"For a man who didn't want to tell me anything, you've said an awful lot," Dana quipped. She paused. "Johnny and Camille are letting Violet get away with doing this in their neighborhood?"

"I don't think they know how big it's gotten. They live in the suburbs and aren't in touch with the happenings around here, like they used to be. I reckon they believed that as long as Violet had a little bit of the action, she wouldn't cause trouble. But they never would let her get away with what's she's doing if they knew the truth."

"Who's helping Violet McCarthy? She can't be on her own."

"Her boyfriend's with her."

"His name?"

"I don't remember his name, but they run *McBurney's*, you know, the pub down the street? I see them in there together all the time."

"Any idea who their supplier is?" Dana asked.

Joseph shrugged. "I got no fucking clue."

"I'll check what you told me," Dana replied, unsure whether to believe him, when she hadn't a reason not to before, and also thinking that she might stop by there after she'd finished here.

Joseph sipped his coffee.

"Hurry up," she told him, so she could pay, as she always did.

Joseph gulped down the rest. "Same time and place next week?" he asked.

Dana put some money on the table and rose from her seat. "Maybe," she said, getting on her jacket.

"Maybe what?"

"It depends on if I need something from you," she told him with a tinge of sarcasm in her voice and slight smile on her face.

"It's nice to know how you think of me," Joseph said, but he knew the score, and that she had the upper hand, and so he thanked her.

"No problem," Dana replied, leaving the diner after him.

3

Dana walked outside, to find the day warmer, but at the lunchtime hour, the city was filled with more noise than when she'd entered the diner. Dana walked quickly, as she felt a lot of pressure to solve this case, and solve it fast, from the higher ups in the police. There were many overdoses in the neighborhood, and people wanted someone to be held accountable. Dana made her way to the place Joseph had mentioned, *McBurney's* pub. She stepped under the green awning. Outside it was bright, but when she opened the heavy wooden door to the pub, she walked into cool darkness. The place hadn't appeared crowded from the street, but inside it was packed with lunch customers, mostly groups of workmen enjoying a chat with each other along with a sandwich and beer. The interior was worn, with fraying decorations on the walls, and a cracked mirror behind the faded wood bar. It didn't exactly seem like the kind of place that attracted an upscale clientele, and if the owners were making big money from dealing smack, it wasn't obvious, but perhaps they were saving their money.

The bartender, a handsome, middle-aged blond man,

noticed her straightaway, and seemed to notice that she didn't belong there.

"Can I help you?" he asked her.

"Are the owners around?" she asked, showing him her badge, wondering if he was the boyfriend Joseph had mentioned.

"Can I ask, what's this about?" the man said with a slight smile. He seemed more educated than she would have thought, and she reasoned he must have done something else before becoming a bartender.

"Are they here?" Dana asked, again.

"I'm one of them," the man finally said.

"Your name?"

"Sam Paul," he said, but didn't offer to shake her hand.

He seemed a bit nervous, and Dana made a mental note to run his name through their computer records at the station.

"What's the name of the other owner?" she asked him.

He hesitated, then seemed to grasp that she wouldn't leave without it. "Violet," he said.

"Violet what?"

"McCarthy," he said after a pause.

So, this was one of the big-time dealers in the neighborhood that Joseph had mentioned. Sam didn't dress the part, but, then again, they didn't always.

"What are you looking for?" Sam asked her, seeming bolder.

"Is Violet around?" Dana asked, ignoring his question.

"Not at the moment, no. What do you want?" he asked her, seeming annoyed, or worried, she couldn't tell which one.

"Nothing," Dana said, turning to leave. It wasn't as though she could outright ask them to confess, but she had applied a little pressure. Putting the heat on a suspect often got them to make an unwise move, to her benefit.

She left the pub, reasoning that Sam would be the easier one of the pair to crack. Of course, she could have been wrong, but she almost never was.

Dana headed to the neighborhood police station to meet the officer who had been assigned to assist her with the case, someone who apparently was very familiar with the neighborhood. Dana didn't like having help, she preferred to work on her own, but she figured she could let them help her and take all the credit.

Inside the station, she exchanged pleasantries and a few jokes with some of the officers, then went to the desk where she'd been given space to work. She sat down and researched Sam Paul and Violet McCarthy, finding that Sam, an ex-banker, had a criminal record for white-collar crime. She couldn't find any criminal convictions for Violet but from what the informant had told her, Sam might have had book smarts, but Violet had street smarts, and in gangland New York that counted for a lot. They were an odd pair, and she wondered how they'd gotten together, but in New York, anything was possible. Dana reasoned that Sam must have been in charge of their operation.

She printed Sam's record and mugshot then took them with her for a meeting with Lieutenant Andrews in his office.

On her way to the meeting, she stopped at the coffee machine to get a cup. She waited behind a tall man in a police uniform for him to finish getting his coffee.

He glanced at her over his shoulder. "Sorry, I seem to be taking forever."

From what she could see, he was young and handsome, with dark good looks, a charming smile, and an easy, carefree demeanor. She was immediately drawn to him.

"That's okay," she said, and found herself giving him a smile, something she rarely did.

"Do you work here?" he turned around and asked her, with

his coffee in hand. She now saw that he had a small scar above his eye, as if he'd been a professional fighter.

"Yeah, I just started here recently. I was just about to go to a meeting—"

"What do you take in your coffee?" he asked her.

"Milk, no sugar," she replied, wondering where this was going.

"Here, take mine; it's how you like it," he said, handing her the warm cup. "This way, you won't be late for your meeting."

"Thanks," she said, and accepted the cup, somewhat flustered by his kindness.

"What's your name?" he asked her.

"I'm Dana," she said, shaking his hand, which felt rough and warm.

"Tommy," he said, waiting a moment to release her hand.

"I should be going," she said, remembering the meeting. "Thanks again for the coffee."

Dana could feel his eyes on her as she walked away, and, for once, she enjoyed the feeling of a strange man looking at her.

Dana entered the lieutenant's office and was surprised when the same man from earlier, Tommy, joined them a few moments later.

"This is Officer Carmine," Lieutenant Andrews said. He seemed to notice the looks exchanged between them. "You two have already met?"

"We have, sir," Tommy said, smiling at Dana.

Dana was unable to hide her disappointment, and nearly frowned. It was hard enough to meet dating prospects in her line of work, as a lot of men weren't attracted to tough lady cops, but Tommy had seemed like a potential match, and now she found out they would be working together, with him under her supervision, which made him off limits, in a way.

"Detective Fitzpatrick has been brought in to help with the

heroin case I told you about. She's in charge of it," Andrews told Tommy. "Tommy's going to be working with you," he said to Dana.

She nodded, and took his words as a cue to show Tommy what she'd printed. Tommy seemed to sense that her demeanor toward him had changed when she didn't return the smile he gave her. She opened the folder and motioned for him to look at the collected papers. Tommy, standing so close to her, smelled of aftershave, and gave her a feeling of warmth.

"This is who my informant suggests are behind it," Dana told him. "Only the one has a record so this is all I have for now. I've asked research to come up with a shot of his partner."

Tommy remained silent for so long that Dana said to him, "Officer Carmine?" His face had paled in such a way that he looked ill.

"Officer Carmine, are you okay?" she asked him when he stayed quiet. "Officer Carmine?"

4

Tommy had gone into the meeting with a plan to tell the lead detective about the likelihood of Camille O'Brien running the heroin operation. To say that the sight of his mother's boyfriend in Detective Fitzpatrick's files shocked him would be a gross understatement. Sam being involved had to mean his mother was as well, with her most likely being in charge. Tommy felt like he would pass out. He couldn't breathe, and he needed air, fast.

"Excuse me," he said, "I don't feel well." He hurried out of the room, with Lieutenant Andrews asking if he was okay.

Outside on the station steps, it took him a moment to realize that Dana had followed him.

"Are you all right?" she asked him, with that file still in her hand.

"Yeah, I'm fine. I just needed some air," he replied.

"You look like you'd seen a ghost in there," Dana said.

Tommy shook his head in denial. "No, it's just that I must've eaten something bad for lunch."

"You seemed okay at the coffee machine earlier," Dana said, in a motherly way, and he felt like he'd known her for a long time. Straight away, he'd been attracted to her, and she seemed genuinely concerned for him, not suspicious.

Dana walked farther outside and stood next to him in silence, seeming to sense his need for solitude.

"I told Lieutenant Andrews I would check on you," she said after a while.

"Is he pissed I just bolted like that?" Tommy asked.

"No, I think he believes you're ill."

Something about the way she said it worried him. "And you don't believe I am?" he asked.

"I'm not sure," Dana said with a slight smile on her pretty face, pushing a sheaf of her soft-looking blonde hair behind her ear.

"I'm not surprised, since you're a detective," Tommy joked.

Her green eyes lit up when she laughed.

"We're going to be working closely with one another," she said, "and I don't want us to get off on the wrong foot. From the way you reacted in there, I thought that maybe you knew something about the case, something you wanted to tell me, perhaps?"

Tommy's mother had claimed to be reformed, with her past behind her, and he'd thought she was just running the pub with Sam, but now he knew she was up to her old tricks.

"No, there's nothing to tell," Tommy replied to Dana in a calm voice, feeling conflicted. His work meant the world to him, but he loved his mother. He knew he would have to make a tough decision. "I really just felt ill," he added when Dana continued to watch him.

Dana nodded and opened the file in front of him. "Are you all right to discuss the case now? Andrews wants us to get started on it right away."

Tommy tried not to wince, for he didn't want to see the

mugshot of Sam again, but he said to Dana, "Sure, I'm fine," and hoped she didn't sense his apprehension.

Standing so close to Dana, she smelled of a flowery perfume, and although he was drawn to her scent and her beauty, he was very much aware of the damage she could do to his mother.

"We need to find their supplier," Dana told him. "My informant claims to not know who it is."

"Do you think he's lying?" Tommy asked. "It's a he, right?"

"Yeah, it's a guy. I'm not sure if he's lying, but he doesn't seem clever enough to lie."

"You think that this Violet McCarthy heads the operation?" Tommy asked, feeling guilty for lying, but he did so out of loyalty to his mother.

"No, I think that Sam Paul is in charge. He's a white-collar criminal type, university educated. McCarthy's got street smarts, but I doubt she has the brains to run such a discreet operation."

Tommy kept his thoughts to himself about how wrong she was. "What are you planning to do?" he asked, worried about his mother's fate. In truth, he'd never liked Sam much, but knew his mother loved him, so he didn't want anything to happen to him either. Tommy would do anything for his mother, but would he risk his entire career, and possibly his future, for her?

"I've already been to their pub," Dana said. "I've put the heat on them."

"You saw both of them?"

"No, just Sam."

Tommy knew he ought to warn his mother before Dana got any closer, but could he?

5

The day after Camille attended Mrs. Valeria's birthday party with Johnny and Phoebe, her mother, Sheila, came over to Camille and Johnny's house in the suburbs for a visit. Sheila sat at the kitchen table while Camille made coffee. She had a plan she wanted to discuss with her mother, but needed to wait until the right moment to propose it.

"So, how have you been?" Camille asked, as she set down two cups of freshly made coffee on the table.

"I'm well. Eric's well," Sheila said, as Camille took in the sight of her tall, strong mother, older now, and more beautiful than ever.

"And Mickey?" Camille asked the name of her stepbrother.

"Not sure," Sheila replied, taking a sip of coffee. "He hasn't been by to see us in a while. But I assume he's okay, I haven't heard otherwise." She paused. "You and Johnny are good?"

"Yeah, we are," Camille answered truthfully. The road to their marriage hadn't been without bumps, but she did feel they were in a good place currently.

"You're a saint for taking that woman's daughter under your wing," Sheila said, and Camille knew she meant Phoebe.

"Don't say that," she said to her mother quietly so that Phoebe wouldn't hear upstairs. "I'm no saint. It's an honor to be a mother to her."

"Still, there aren't many women who would do that, another woman's child."

"I love that girl as my own," Camille replied. She wasn't one to scold her own mother, but enough was enough. Sheila brought Phoebe up nearly every time she visited, when the girl was out of earshot. Camille had always thought of herself as having a good relationship with her mother, but she resented Shelia's attitude.

"You won't be welcome in this house again if you keep this up," she told her mother.

Sheila put down her coffee cup and put her hand to her chest and acted shocked. "You never used to speak that way to me. You've changed, Camille."

She had changed. She'd become a wife and a mother. Her own mother hadn't liked Johnny at first either, but had grown to accept their relationship over the years, and they'd reached a place of understanding, for the most part. She loved her mother, and still considered her family, but Johnny and Phoebe had become her main family.

"I'm sorry, but that's the way it is," Camille said, then because she needed to ask her mother for a favor, she added, "You know I love you," with a smile, as she sat down at the table.

Sheila wasn't one to easily back down, but she did appreciate affection, especially from her only daughter. "I love you, too, honey." But, because she also knew her daughter very well, she asked, "What do you want this time?"

Camille laughed slightly, for her mother knew her all too well. "I know you've taken a backseat to the business since your marriage to Eric, but Johnny and I have got a problem on our hands, and we need to deal with it quickly."

"Who is it this time?" Sheila asked.

Sheila was well-schooled in the gangland world, as Camille's father was a gangster, and Sheila's second husband was in the Italian mafia. So, mother and daughter talked 'business' as easily as making plans for a party.

"Violet McCarthy. Who else?" Camille said bitterly.

"I thought she wasn't giving you trouble anymore, after that deal we reached."

"Turns out, we never should've done that. You know how that family is—they want to get their fucking claws on everything."

"I never liked that little bitch. I can't believe you were ever friends with her," Sheila said.

Camille shrugged off the remark from her mother. "We were never really friends, just knew each other." Camille had once worked at the pub Violet and her mother owned. "Anyway, remember how we let her have a little piece of the action to get her off our backs? She isn't behaving. She's running her own dope ring now, and it's getting bigger by the day."

"How'd you find this out?" Sheila asked.

"Anton."

"Fucking Anton," her mother said, shaking her head.

"No," Camille said. "Anton told me. He's got no part in it."

"So he says," Sheila remarked.

"No, I trust him," she said, and she really did.

"Johnny knows?" Sheila asked.

"Of course."

"What does he think?"

"I dunno; he's been kind of quiet about it. He's thinking."

"Tell him to think faster."

"He's my husband, and I respect his opinion, but I came up with my own plan."

"You talk to him about it?"

"Not yet," Camille said, and braced herself for her mother's disapproval.

"You always were an independent woman, but Johnny's your man, and his opinion is important."

Camille sighed and drank her coffee. "He and I will talk soon. I promise," she said to get her mother to back down.

"When?" Sheila goaded.

"Soon."

"So, what's this great plan of yours that you haven't told him about?" her mother asked with a smile. "But first, more coffee." She gestured for Camille to refill her cup.

Camille rose and went over to the pot on the counter and poured her mother another cup. Then she sat down again.

"I'm listening," Sheila said between sips of coffee.

For the first time in her life, Camille hesitated to tell her mother what was on her mind. They had always been very close, and she knew her mother supported her, no matter what, but Camille's plan might change that.

"I need you to hurt me," she said, somewhat quietly.

Sheila put down her cup and just stared at Camille. "What?" she said, after a moment.

"I need you to, you know, beat me up."

Shelia's jaw dropped. "What the hell for?"

"So that I can say Violet McCarthy did it, then she goes to jail and her operation stops."

"Why not just kill her?" Sheila asked after a moment of silence.

"I've thought about that," Camille said, sipping her coffee, "and I'm worried about who would take her place. You know the saying, the devil you know is better than one you don't. She'll be in jail, and her racket would stop growing 'cause her guy, Sam whatever-the-fuck-his-name-is, he's not capable of running it on his own. So it'd stop, but no one would dare take her place while she's still breathing."

"There's some truth in what you say," Sheila mused. "Camille, sweetheart, you know I'd do anything for you, I have ever since you were born, but this? This is madness."

"No," Camille said, carefully, "it's love. Can't you see? It'd be out of love. If you do this for me, then she's gone from our lives for good. I can just feel it."

"Sure, they'd send her away for a couple of years. Then what? She gets out and is up to her old tricks, and you got to deal with her again."

"It'd be aggravated assault. They could send her away for twenty-five years, maybe more. You got to admit, it'd buy us a lot of time. After you do it, you'd drop me off near the hospital and I'd stumble in and say Violet beat me."

"Aggravated assault. That's pretty serious. I'd have to hurt you bad. I wouldn't want to damage that nice face of yours."

"I put one of our guys on her trail, and Violet does a supply run to get milk in the morning on Mondays, and she takes a shortcut through the alley behind her pub," Camille said, continuing to tell her mother the plan despite Sheila's resistance.

"Jesus, Camille, have you not heard a damn word I've said?" Sheila swiped at the coffee cup and some spilled on the table.

Camille shot up from her chair and grabbed a cloth to wipe the mess. Then, with her back turned to her mother, she pretended to cry, as her showing emotion always seemed to get to Sheila.

After a moment, Sheila reached over and put her hand over Camille's. "Is this really so important to you?" she asked quietly.

With her back still turned, Camille nodded.

Sheila sighed. "I'll do it. But only because I love you."

Camille quickly turned and hugged her mother. "I love you," she said. "You'd do anything for me."

"When do you need me to do it by?" Sheila asked.

"I was planning to do it tonight."

Sheila nodded. "One thing," she said, as Camille started to sit down to finish her coffee. "Johnny's got to be okay with our plan. He's got to know about it, you can't keep something like that from your husband."

"Of course," Camille said. She'd planned to tell Johnny all along, but wasn't sure how. Johnny wouldn't want to see her hurt, and would do anything to stop it, but at the same time, she knew he'd want to protect their assets.

"When?" Sheila pushed her for an answer. "When are you going to tell him?"

"Soon."

"Soon? Sweetie, you want me to do this tonight. Soon is not going to cut it. Better do it fast. Where is he now?"

Johnny was in their garage, working on one of their luxury cars. Another reason they liked living in the suburbs, because they could hide their money from the city cops.

Camille contemplated whether to lie to her mother, then said, "He's outside."

"Better hurry up and tell him before your coffee gets cold," Sheila said, gently pushing on Camille's back to get her to leave.

The gesture made her feel like a child again, and, like a child, she followed her mother's orders.

She opened the side door to the garage and then hesitated as she approached Johnny, who had his back turned to her as he worked on a hot red car. She knew her plan would anger him, and she didn't want Phoebe upstairs to hear them arguing.

"Johnny?" she said quietly, and he turned to look at her.

"What's going on, baby?" The tall, handsome Johnny, with his dark good looks, smiled as he wiped grease from his hands with a small towel. "Is your mother gone yet?" he teased, because he was actually fond of her mother now, despite the two having had a previously tense relationship.

"She's still here," Camille said, and almost smiled, until she remembered what she came to tell him.

Johnny stepped close to her and reached out to touch her face, but she stopped him and looked at his hands for grease.

"They're clean," he said, with a smile, holding them up for her to see.

Camille nodded and he lightly stroked her face and kissed her, but she had too much on her mind and didn't delight in his touch. She needed to tell him her plan, and she needed to do it fast. She hadn't asked Johnny to be part of her plan, because she knew he wouldn't want to hurt her. But she couldn't lie to him, because he'd be angry if he found out she had. Her mother was right about that. Close couples didn't keep secrets from each other, not even this.

"Johnny," she said as he continued to touch her face, stepping away from him.

"What's wrong?" he asked, with his brow furrowed.

"It's nothing you did," Camille assured him. "It's something I've been discussing with my mother. I think I've thought of a way to get rid of Violet McCarthy that doesn't involve us risking being locked up."

"Go on, tell me," Johnny said, with his sexy half smile.

"It's my idea, but my mother's going to help." Camille took a deep breath.

Johnny sensed her apprehension and said, "C, is everything okay?"

"You're going to think I'm crazy, but, my mother, she's going to hurt me and then I'm going to make it look like Violet did it," Camille said quickly, so that she wouldn't be tempted to leave without telling him the truth.

Johnny's gaze narrowed on her. "Hurt you? How?" he asked, stepping close to her, so that she was forced to meet his eyes with hers.

"She's going to beat me up," Camille said, quietly.

"No, that's insane. There must be a better way."

"Like what?" Camille said in exasperation, as the light from outside poured through the garage window and shone in her face. "I've thought of everything, and this is the only way we get to keep the business, stay out of jail, and get rid of her."

"Why don't we just kill her?"

"No," Camille said.

"Why the hell not," Johnny said, his face flushing red. "We've done that to so many others. One more won't make a difference."

"I already talked with my mother about this, and who would replace Violet? Somebody worse? You know the saying, *The enemy you know…*"

"Yeah, I do," Johnny said, as he put his hand to his head and sighed. "I don't like anyone hurting you, even your own mother," he said, looking at her, reaching out and putting his arms around her waist. He tugged her closer to him. "Don't do this," he said, and his gaze darkened as he warned her. "If you do, Phoebe and I might have to leave."

"Are you threatening me?" Camille asked, recoiling from his hold on her.

"Yeah, maybe I am. Because I care about you," he said, moving to touch her face.

Camille allowed him to, for a moment, because she knew his anger well and feared it. Then she looked away from him. "I'm going to do it anyway," she whispered.

"Business means more to you than we do?" Johnny said, his voice rising.

"No, of course not. You know how much I love you," she said, her voice tightening as she fought back emotion. "But this is the only way. I can feel it in my gut."

A moment of silence fell between them, with Camille's stomach tensing as she wondered, and dreaded, how Johnny would react.

"How badly does your mother have to hurt you?" Johnny asked, after a while, as though he still didn't like the idea but could come around to it because he loved her—and wanted to protect their business.

Camille exhaled with relief that she would avoid his wrath this time. "Badly enough for them to put that bitch away for a long time," she answered carefully, her face heating with anger at the mention of Violet.

"She's going to use, what, her fists, or something heavy?"

"My mother's an older lady, but you and I both know she's stronger than me. She's going to knock me about, and she might even enjoy doing it, after all the shit she's had to put up with from me over the years." Camille laughed a little and managed to get a smile out of Johnny.

"Come here," he said, reaching to hold her, and she walked into his strong arms. "I still don't like the idea."

Even as she was walking into the garage, she debated whether to tell him at all. Camille looked up at him. She knew her mother wouldn't go through with it unless Johnny was onboard, after her remark about not going against your husband. But how could she convince him?

She wiggled her way out of his arms and slowly knelt in front of him on the floor. She grabbed his pants by the waist and undid the button, as he twisted his fingers through her hair and held her face close to him.

6

The evening of the following day, Camille sat in the chair in the cold, dim garage, the chair that her mother had tied her to so she wouldn't be tempted to fight back, instinctively. Sheila had put about 30 heavy coins in a pillowcase and took another swing at Camille's face. They had to make it look real, and so it hurt like fucking hell. Camille started to duck then forced herself to accept the blow across her cheekbone. Her face stung and she could feel blood dribbling down her cheek.

It was only the second hit.

"Oh, sweetheart, I am so sorry," Sheila said softly, yet there was a glimmer of pleasure in her eyes that made Camille think her mother was enjoying it a little too much. Perhaps it was a form of revenge for Camille's moody teenage years.

"Just a couple more, and then we're done," Sheila said as Camille moaned from another strike, across her forehead this time.

"No, make it look real. I can take it," Camille said, her voice hoarse with pain. Thinking of Violet locked away for years, maybe even more, maybe life, helped her get through the ordeal.

Johnny had taken Phoebe out to dinner, to get her out of the house. Then he planned to drop her off at her friend's house after, to spend the night. Johnny had told Camille it was for Phoebe's sake, so that she wouldn't overhear the commotion, but Camille sensed it was for Johnny's sake as well, so that he would refrain from throttling her mother for hurting her.

Her mother nodded and prepared to take another blow. They had set a few rules beforehand: they had to make it appear real, but the injuries could be nothing that really damaged Camille. The eyes, ears, legs and arms were off limits, but elsewhere on the face, and the chest, made for a disturbing visual effect, which Camille wanted.

They'd planned for Sheila to drive Camille into the city when it was over, and drop her off near the hospital by Violet's pub. Johnny would get rid of the evidence at their town's garbage center, where he had a friend. Camille had had a few shots of strong Irish whiskey beforehand to lessen the pain.

Camille turned her head away when Sheila hit her mouth with the heavy coins. She could feel her lip split open and warm blood gushing out down to her shirt and she looked down as it absorbed into and spread across the white fabric. She'd worn white on purpose, so that it would highlight the blood. Camille coughed as her mother smacked the pillowcase across her chest, lightly enough so that it wouldn't kill her, but hard enough so that it'd leave a mark on Camille's skin.

Half an hour later sweat dripped from Sheila's brow as she breathed out. "Phew," she said. "This is quite a workout."

Camille knew her mother was trying to make light of a strange situation, but her body ached and burned from the wounds and the bleeding, and she called for her mother to stop.

"Bring the mirror over to me," she said, her throat dry. "And some water."

Sheila dropped the pillow with the coins in it on the floor and got the items. She held up the mirror to Camille's face, and

Camille let out a long gasp. Her mother had done a good job, perhaps a little too good. Sheila hadn't done so much damage that Camille would be maimed for life, but it looked as though it would take some time to heal, and it would be a while before Johnny desired her again.

"Untie me, so I can drink," Camille said, trying to reach for the water in her mother's hand, but unable to.

Sheila walked behind her and quickly undid the cord. She held out the water to Camille, who took it and drank.

"Slowly, honey," Sheila told her daughter.

Camille didn't heed her mother's advice and gulped the water down. Her mother started to hand her a cloth to wipe her face but Camille stopped her.

"No, I don't want to clean the blood, we need to make it look real, we need the police to believe me," she said in a raspy voice.

Sheila nodded and put the cloth away. She helped Camille stand up from the chair and the pain hit Camille all at once. Seated, it hadn't been so bad, but standing, it felt like every inch of her body had taken the beating. She throbbed and burned, and her stomach churned as she suppressed a gag.

"I'll drive you to the city," Sheila said. When Camille didn't answer her, Sheila said, "Camille, are you going to be okay? You're my daughter, my girl, I hate to just drop you off and leave."

"There's no other way. You can come later. When they ask to ring a family member, I'll give your name. Then you can call Johnny. Don't bring Phoebe to the hospital. I don't want her seeing me like this."

"Honey, she's going to have to see you eventually," Sheila said.

"I don't want to think about that now. Let's just get this over with."

Sheila handed Camille her purse and went outside to check

that the neighbors were out of sight. When it was clear, she helped Camille out of the garage to her car in the lighted driveway. Sheila got her seated in the back of the car, and then sat in the driver's seat.

"Take your time," Camille told her mother. "Wouldn't want you to get stopped by the cops." She made a light joke, and could see her mother smiling slightly in the rearview mirror.

Sheila left the driveway toward the highway.

"Music?" her mother asked out on the quiet road.

"Sure."

A pop singer's soft voice filled the car, and the sound made Camille's eyelids flutter. She straightened when she started to fall asleep, and looked out the window at the passing scenery: the occasional other car, identical, polished suburban houses, and a well-lit restaurant. Ordinary things, but they made Camille feel out of place, the house especially, because she knew she didn't belong in the pristine town. She was a tough, city girl, a gritty girl, a career criminal, who the hell was she trying to fool, living in the suburbs? Ever since moving there, she'd tried her best to fit in, but knew that most of the other people who lived there, the other parents at Phoebe's school especially, viewed her as an outsider, and probably always would, as someone with a rough accent and a Latin husband. At least she wasn't stuck in their old, shitty neighborhood, like Violet was. That brought a small, painful smile to Camille's face, despite the circumstances.

The traffic thickened once they neared Manhattan, and Camille's pulse quickened. She could feel the blood on her skin starting to dry. What the hell would she tell the doctors at the hospital, that she'd stopped to have a smoke after she was beaten?

"You're going to have to take a shortcut, Ma," she told her mother.

"You're right, baby," Sheila replied, then maneuvered out of their lane and pressed down on the accelerator toward a side street, leaving a beeping chorus of the other cars in her wake.

"Fuck you!" Sheila shouted at the top of her lungs.

"Jesus, Ma, that was fucking loud," Camille said.

"Sorry, I can't help myself. It's those rude assholes that bother me," Sheila said.

They neared Violet's neighborhood, which belonged to Camille and Johnny, and Camille hoped that her mother's red Mercedes, which Camille had given her as a present, wouldn't be recognized by any potential witnesses. Not that anyone in the neighborhood would dare squeal on anyone in her family. Everyone knew much better than that. Squealers, rats, got cut. Killed.

Sheila made sure no police were around, and then parked in a fog-filled alleyway by the hospital. She left the engine running when she exited the car to help Camille out. Sheila opened the passenger door and Camille eased her sore body out of the seat.

"Leave, Ma," she ordered her mother. "We don't need any cops seeing you and then start sniffing around."

"I hate leaving you like this," Sheila replied.

"It's part of the plan," Camille said.

Sheila hesitated for a moment longer, then nodded, and got into the car. Camille watched her mother driving off then emerged from thick fog to walk toward the hospital, a tall, white building, which she could see in the distance. She stumbled across the street, and a taxi swerved out of her way.

"Watch where you're going, lady," a man shouted at her from the car, but Camille clutched her chest and staggered forward, too tired to react.

She reached the hospital and pushed past a group of young people smoking by the entrance. They seemed like they were waiting for someone inside.

"What the fuck is wrong with her?" one of them said. "Girl looks messed up."

The automatic doors opened and Camille shuffled inside, dropping to her knees on the cold, hard floor once the glare of the indoor lights hit her eyes.

A woman wearing a crisp white uniform shouted in her direction. A nurse?

Through blurry eyes, Camille could see the people seated in the waiting room watching her. Then she closed her eyes as she collapsed to the floor, hearing the sound of a stretcher being wheeled toward her as she pretended to lose consciousness.

What happened next Camille could only hear as she kept her eyes shut. Someone, a man, she thought, pulled her off the floor onto the stretcher.

"Looks like somebody beat the shit out of her," she heard him say. She assumed he was a hospital attendant.

"Let's get her seen by a doctor, ASAP," the nurse said. "We'll move her to the front of the line. Thank God, there's only one gunshot victim so far tonight."

Camille could feel them watching her and struggled to keep her eyes closed. Then she felt the stretcher being rolled away. She groaned a little, and it wasn't pretend, as she really did feel awful.

"Has she got any ID on her?" she heard the nurse ask the attendant. "A wallet, maybe? She doesn't have a purse on her."

"Let me check," he said. She felt the stretcher stop and him going through her pockets.

She had her wallet tucked inside the pocket of her jeans and could feel him pulling it out.

"Name's Camille Garcia," he told the nurse.

"Any next of kin listed anywhere?"

Camille felt them resume pushing her and heard what sounded like a curtain being closed around her.

"No," the man said to the woman. "I'll have one of the girls ring the police while you get her set up."

Camille could feel and hear the nurse checking her vitals, then what sounded like another man, a doctor, speaking to the nurse. She heard him mentioning something about her needing X-rays and pondering about possible trauma to her brain. At that, Camille's eyes shot open. She wasn't going to allow anybody to poke around her fucking brain.

"Doctor, she's awake," the nurse, who Camille now saw was a pretty, blonde woman, who looked younger than she'd sounded.

"Ms. Garcia," the doctor, a tall, older, white-haired man, said. "Ms. Garcia, can you hear me?"

Camille wondered whether she should lie to make her injuries seem worse than they were, but they probably would figure it out, so she held back.

"Ms. Garcia, did someone do this to you?" he asked her. "We rang the police."

Camille nodded. "I saw who did it," she spoke weakly. "I know the person. Her name's Violet McCarthy, and it happened out on the street just now, I..." She feigned struggling.

The doctor calmed her. "It's all right; you don't have to talk just now. The police will want to speak with you when they arrive."

Camille nodded and shut her eyes again, though she wasn't really tired anymore. The excitement of the situation buzzed through her like electricity, and she listened to the sounds of the hospital around her as the doctor and his team worked on her, the sounds of someone coding in another room, and then a woman sobbing, and a child crying. Someone cut off her clothes with what sounded like scissors and then what felt like a gown was wrapped around her. She winced as she could feel something being attached to her chest. A heart monitor? The nurse checked her breathing, then she was giving oxygen, and an IV drip was connected to her arm.

She heard someone, a man, say, "The police are waiting outside."

Then they must have given her some kind of drug to make her relax, because soon she drifted off the sleep.

Camille woke up in her hospital room to see Johnny punching a wall, and hospital security restraining him. Either Johnny was a good actor, or she really did look like shit. At least her mother hadn't broken her nose. Well, at least it didn't feel like she had.

The security guard told Johnny he would have to leave if he couldn't control himself. Johnny nodded quietly, his face flushed red.

A nurse entered the room, and Camille asked Johnny what had happened to her, pretending to be forgetful, as the nurse connected another fluid bag to her IV drip pole.

"Somebody hurt you, baby," Johnny said as he approached her bedside. "The good news is that nothing is broken." He gave her a beautiful smile and smoothed back her hair from her face. Camille nestled into his warm touch and watched her mother coming into the room with two paper cups of what seemed like coffee. She handed one to Johnny and gave Camille a wink, and a look of understanding passed between them.

"Where's Phoebe?" Camille asked Johnny.

"She's with her friend."

"How are you, sweetheart?" her mother asked her. "You still are beautiful."

"I want to see what I look like," Camille said, and the nurse cleared her throat quietly.

"I'm not sure if that's a good idea," Johnny said.

"I can handle it," she replied.

Sheila gave Johnny a look of hesitation, then dug through

her purse, handing Camille her small makeup mirror as the security guard left the room.

Camille took one look at her swollen, purpled face, and shoved the mirror back in her mother's direction. She'd known she'd look bad afterwards, but she hadn't known she'd look *that* bad.

"I certainly don't look beautiful," she joked to her mother with a smile.

A man who looked like a police detective, in a dark suit, entered Camille's room and she sat up, eager to finally be able to speak to the police, and the nurse stepped out of the room.

"I'm Detective Highland," he said as he approached her bedside, and reached out to shake her hand. "I hear that you'd like to report an assault committed against you?"

Camille nodded as she smiled and shook the tall, chubby, red-haired man's hand.

7

Violet stood at the stove and put the pasta in the boiling water, as she made spaghetti with meatballs in a red sauce for Sam and herself, when she heard a knock, or more like a pounding, on the door.

"What the fuck?" she muttered to herself. "Sam?" she called to him in the other room where he watched television.

"I'll get it," he replied, and she heard him rising from the couch.

Sam opened the door and Violet could hear him talking to someone, or more like, some people. And they sounded like cops. Violet knew the sound of the police well, with that authoritative note in their voices, like they knew they could smack you around and you couldn't do anything about it. And, hell, they could. But Tommy was a cop, so they must not all have been bad. Well, at least Tommy wasn't.

Violet turned off the stove and searched her memories for the latest illegal activity she'd done. Oh, yeah, the heroin dealing. But these cops hadn't come bursting through the door with their guns drawn, so it didn't look like a drug bust. So, what the fuck did they want?

"Ms. McCarthy?" the tall, red-haired man in the suit said, as she approached the small, narrow hallway from the kitchen. "I need to talk to you." The guy, stood in the doorway, flanked by two police officers, whose faces she couldn't see, as Sam held the door open.

Violet didn't even need the tall man to introduce himself for her to know he was a detective.

"What's this about?" Sam asked for her.

"It's about an assault that's been committed," he replied in a solemn tone.

What kind of fucking nonsense was this? Violet thought to herself. She hadn't beaten anyone in quite a while, and neither had any of her guys, from what she knew.

He introduced himself as Detective Highland and then she begrudgingly allowed them into her living room.

The two uniform cops, a younger man and an older woman, quietly stood by as though they were waiting for the detective's orders like obedient dogs. They were there as backup, and Violet knew that.

"Am I under arrest?" she asked the detective, with Sam at her side, holding her hand, which she suspected comforted him more than it did her.

"We need to speak with you," he said, not answering her question. "You'll need to come with us to the station."

"She hasn't done anything," Sam said in her defense.

Detective Highland ignored him and said to Violet, "We need you to come with us now."

"It's not like I have a choice," Violet said, eyeing the two uniformed officers near him who had stepped closer, as though they were prepared to restrain her if she lashed out.

"I'll go with you," Sam told her, with a concerned gaze.

"No, honey, you haven't eaten dinner, and this'll probably

take a few hours. Right?" She looked to the cops, using her sweetest concerned partner voice.

Highland nodded.

"What station are we going to?" she suddenly asked him, hoping it wasn't Tommy's, as she didn't want to embarrass him.

He gave her the name of one that wasn't her son's, and she exhaled in relief.

"Are you sure?" Sam asked her, again, as she collected her purse and jacket from the hallway. "I don't like the idea of you going alone."

"I'll be fine, call Jake," she said, accustomed to the routine of talking with the police. "Don't worry, I'll be fine. Once I get to the station, I'm not opening my damn mouth until he's there." Violet kept their lawyer, Jake, on a retainer for things like this.

Sam kissed her goodbye. "I'll finish dinner."

"Sweetheart, you don't have to," Violet said as she stroked his face.

"No, it's fine, I'll do it."

Violet kissed him again then said to the detective with a smirk, "Aren't you going to cuff me?"

He glanced at the two other officers. "I don't think that's needed, do you?"

Violet shrugged. She didn't feel much like joking with a cop. "Just so you know, when we get there, I'm not talking to you until my lawyer gets there."

"Of course you aren't," the detective replied, sarcasm thick in his voice.

"I hope this won't take too long. I haven't had dinner yet."

She left the apartment with Detective Highland and the two police officers, and followed them down the stairs to a police car parked outside on the street. A few of her neighbors waved to her and didn't so much as give a second glance. The sight was normal in the community. Violet smiled and waved back to them.

"Tell me what this is about," Violet said to Detective Highland ahead of her.

He didn't reply. She kept asking him, and he kept saying, "Down at the station."

Once inside the car, "What? You aren't going to put on the sirens?" Violet quipped to the female officer seated next to her in the back.

Detective Highland overheard her from the front, where he sat with the male officer, who drove the car.

"We can't put them on just for you," he said.

Had he made another joke? Perhaps her interrogation wouldn't be so dull after all.

The car stopped and they were stuck in traffic for a few minutes. Then they continued on, and soon they reached the police station. Violet knew the routine by heart. The cops parked in a special area reserved for bringing in suspects, then she followed them inside the ordinary brick building. This time, no fingerprints were taken, and she was escorted directly into an interrogation room and told to sit at the table. Whatever the hell this was about, they wanted to get it done immediately. Detective Highland sat across from her without offering her a coffee or something to drink first, and so Violet knew this was serious. She expected that Sam had rung her lawyer and he would arrive very soon.

"So, are you going to tell me what this is about, or what?" she said.

"Somebody said you assaulted them," he replied coolly.

Violet sat back in her chair and made a face. "What? That's bullshit. I didn't do nothing. Who the hell said this? No, wait, I want my lawyer here."

Highland cleared his throat. "Very well." He didn't move, and she wondered if he'd spend the whole time waiting for her lawyer to arrive staring at her.

Violet searched through her purse, which one of the officers had searched before, for a piece of gum, anything, to distract her while she waited. She didn't like him looking at her, it made her a little nervous, and, normally, cops didn't make her nervous. But there was something about Detective Highland that spelled trouble. Even though, this time, she hadn't done anything wrong, she couldn't help feel on edge.

After what felt like a long time sitting in silence in the small room, the door opened and her lawyer, Jake Precise, entered, trailed by a young-looking male uniformed cop.

"Do you need anything, sir?" the cop asked Detective Highland.

"No, we're fine," he told the guy.

Violet knew there had to have been other detectives watching from the other side of the mirror behind her.

Jake greeted Violet and sat down next to her. "I'd like a few minutes alone with my client," he told Detective Highland, who nodded firmly and rose.

Violet waited until he'd exited to tell Jake, "What the hell is this all about? Have they said anything?"

"Camille Garcia was assaulted and she's told the police that you were the assailant."

"When did this happen?" Violet said, too shocked to process what she'd just been told.

"It was recently."

"She's a fucking liar!" Violet screamed, banging her fists on the table, then standing up and shaking her hands in rage. "I never fucking touched her."

"I'm sure you didn't," Jake said, with a touch of irony in his voice, for all those other times when she hadn't 'really done it', but he'd known she'd had. "Regardless, you know the drill. The police have to take the complaint seriously."

"Are they going to charge me?" Violet said, unable to calm herself enough to sit down again.

"They haven't said."

"Why is she doing this?" Violet asked, more to herself than to Jake. But deep down inside, she knew the answer: Camille must have somehow found out about her heroin dealing. And what did Camille plan to do, send her to jail for life? Probably. Violet sensed Camille's intentions, because although they were enemies, they thought alike.

"No need to tell me," Violet said to Jake. "I think I know the reason."

"What is it?"

"It's not important," Violet said, unwilling to admit to the crime, even in front of her lawyer, and especially not while she was in what she was certain was a room with a recorder. "You just need to know I didn't do this."

"They're going to talk with you, but remember, you don't need to say anything," Jake reminded her.

"Yeah, I know the routine," Violet said. "Let's just get this over with. But I want to make one thing clear: I'm not going to jail over that bitch."

Good lawyer that he was, Jake patted her hand and said, "Don't worry, you'll be fine."

He rose and left the room and came back with Detective Highland, who sat down across from Violet. Jake sat next to her and opened his briefcase, removed a legal pad and pen, and set them on the table.

"Your lawyer has explained why you're here?" the detective asked her.

Violet nodded in silence.

He started asking her questions about her whereabouts and she stopped him. "I haven't seen Camille in ages."

She'd decided to speak to the police because, this time, she really hadn't done anything wrong.

"Are you aware that she's been hospitalized because of the extent of her injuries?"

"I didn't know that, no, but I assumed it. Anyway, I couldn't have done it. I was at the beauty salon getting my hair and nails done."

"They'll confirm this?"

"Of course," Violet said, and gave him the name of the salon.

"Your hands," Detective Highland said.

"What?"

He gestured at her hands. "I need to check them."

Unsure of what to do, Violet looked to Jake for guidance, and he nodded at her to go on.

"I've got nothing to hide," Violet said, shoving her hands close to the detective.

Highland examined her skin with his cold touch, and his hands felt a little too smooth for a man. Violet pulled back from him when she felt he'd spent enough time checking her.

"Find what you were looking for?" she said.

He didn't reply, but she knew he'd found nothing because she had nothing to hide. "No marks, right?" she said, and he stared at her with a frosty gaze. He must have known about her reputation, and Violet could tell he didn't think she was a nice little lady. She didn't fool him one bit.

"If you're done here, I'd like for my client to be able to go home now," Jake interrupted them.

Detective Highland looked at him and simply replied, "All right." Violet could feel his anger as he left the room before them.

"I don't think he'll drop it," she said to Jake when they were alone.

"You told me you have nothing to hide," Jake said, patting her hand. "If that's the case, then you'll be fine."

"It *is* the case," Violet said, not liking that he doubted her, although she'd given him cause to so many times before.

"Let's get you home; I'll drive you," he said.

They walked past Highland standing with an older woman who also looked like a detective near the rows of desks, and Violet could feel their eyes on her as she left the station with Jake at her side. She had a heavy feeling in her heart. She thought of her mother and knew how wrong these things could go.

8

Dana had spent most of the day briefing Tommy on the heroin case, and they had had a long day. So when Tommy suggested they get dinner afterwards, she agreed to it, though her instincts told her not to. She hadn't eaten much that day, but her gut told her that she shouldn't get to know Tommy after hours. Her attraction to him was too strong, and she didn't date co-workers, and especially not those who worked under her. But when Tommy gave a woman that charming smile, there was little she could do to say no.

"Do you want to go to a bar instead?" Tommy asked her as they stood on the station steps, smoking cigarettes before they left.

"I thought you said you wanted to go to dinner," Dana replied. Tommy was younger than her, but at her age she didn't frequent bars that much anymore, much less with a younger man. "I need food, not booze and a headache in the morning."

"I do want to go to dinner, but you do know that they usually have a menu at the bar?"

She knew he was young and probably wanted to unwind after work.

"Fine, I'll go to a bar," she said because he had that smile. She flicked her cigarette to the ground and stomped it out with her foot.

Tommy continued to smoke as they walked and they had a conversation about a new law banning people from smoking cigarettes in pubs.

"Where are we going?" Tommy asked her after they had walked for a few minutes.

"Wait a minute, I thought you had a bar in mind," she said.

He looked at her and shook his head and they started laughing.

Dana looked around the crowded street, searching the shopfronts for a pub. They moved off to the side of the street, away from the middle, so that the impatient pedestrians wouldn't bump into them. The bright city lights illuminated the tired faces around them.

"You've worked here the longest," Dana teased him. "You find a place."

"All right," Tommy said with a smile, looking around. "There's a place at that corner." He gestured to down the street.

"You're sure? You don't sound sure," she teased him.

"I'm sure," he said with a smile, that smile she couldn't resist.

They walked down the street and reached the pub. From the outside, Dana could see that the place was packed with customers and knew she and Tommy would have to wait a while to get a table, or they'd have to sit at the bar. Tommy opened the door for Dana and gestured for her to go inside. Dana went in and the bartender, a big, burly fellow with a headful of black curls, greeted them.

"You're here for dinner or just to drink?" he asked with a toothy grin.

"Dinner," Tommy said, and Dana liked that he'd answered

for them. Typically, she liked to be in control, even with men, but Tommy's charm made her want to give in.

The bartender made a clicking sound with his tongue. "I'm afraid you'll have to wait, then. Unless you wouldn't mind sitting at the bar?"

Just like Dana had thought.

Tommy looked at Dana, who nodded, then he answered for the both of them, "The bar will be fine, thanks."

Dana looked at the crowded bar and didn't know where they would find an empty seat, but the bartender indicated to farther down from where they stood waiting, and Dana noticed two vacant bar stools. Tommy led the way to them, and Dana kept telling herself that they were simply two work colleagues having a drink and a meal after work, nothing more. But one look at Tommy's tall, strong build, and dark, handsome features, made him hard to resist.

They elbowed their way into their seats, and Tommy tried to get the bartender's attention so that he'd bring them a menu. They waited patiently while he finished fulfilling other customers' orders, and he finally reached them.

"What would you like to drink?" he asked them as he set the menu between them on the bar.

"Bring us a bottle of whiskey," Tommy said.

Dana looked at him incredulously. Not only would it set him back a few good dollars, but just how drunk did he want to get?

"Just kidding," Tommy said to Dana with a wink.

And she wanted to slap him. And then grab him and kiss him.

Tommy smiled at her and waited for her to order first, like a true gentleman.

"I'll have a glass of red wine," Dana told the bartender.

"I'll take a beer," Tommy said when it was his turn. "I'm paying," he said to Dana, looking at her.

"No, that's okay."

"It's fine. I've got it," he insisted.

"All right, if it really means that much to you. I think we pay for our drinks and everything at the end, since we'll be ordering food."

The bartender left to make their drinks, and Tommy and Dana looked through the menu together. His hand, warm and rough, brushed past hers as he turned the menu over, and sent a little shiver down her thighs. Tommy looked at her next to him and smiled.

"You said you were hungry, otherwise I'd have asked you to share something," he said.

"You're a cheap date," she teased him, and Tommy grinned at her.

They both ordered sandwiches, and the bartender brought them their drinks first. Usually, Dana had no problem starting a conversation, but with Tommy, it felt different. She had so many things she wanted to ask him, to say to him, that she didn't know where she should begin.

"Why did you become a cop?" she asked him, as she sipped her red wine. She felt so nervous that she wanted to gulp down the whole glass quickly, but restrained herself.

For some reason, Tommy seemed to hesitate.

"There were lots of reasons," he said, drinking his beer.

"Can you tell me one of them?" she asked, unsure what was bothering him.

"To tell you the truth," Tommy said after a pause. "It was because of my father."

"Was he a police officer?"

Tommy shook his head.

"Oh, was he somehow involved with law enforcement?" she asked him.

"You could say that."

It was hard to hear him above the noise in the pub, but she thought she'd heard him right, and it quickly dawned on Dana what he meant. "Oh, was he a criminal?" she said, then she wished she hadn't, but it had come out so quickly.

Tommy nodded slowly, and she admired his honesty.

"Do the guys at work know?" she asked, because that was the first thing that came to her mind.

"We don't really talk about it, but I'm sure they know," Tommy said. "Doesn't matter now, my dad died a long time ago, when I was just a kid."

"I'm so sorry, Tommy," she said, touching his arm in sympathy.

"Thanks."

Dana didn't know what to say next. She'd never really known the child of a criminal before Tommy. She did recall that her mother, Lucille, told her stories about Lucille's gangster friend she had growing up in the city. That was before her mother met her father.

"What did he do, if you don't mind my asking?" Dana said. She had never been good at being subtle, and she assumed Tommy's father must have been a small-time criminal.

"He was involved with some bad characters, there's not much more to say."

But why did she get the feeling there *was* more to say? A lot more. But Tommy had opened up to her, and she sensed he didn't just open up to anyone, so she nodded, noticed her glass was empty, and motioned for the bartender. Both ordered another round of drinks.

"What's your family like?" Tommy suddenly asked her, his face slightly flushed. "I'm sure they're nothing like mine," he said, and she wanted to ask him what he meant, but he'd been so guarded before.

"My dad was a policeman," she said after a moment. "My

mother a housewife. You know, you never told me about your mother."

"You could say my mother has a colorful past," he said, but didn't elaborate.

"Mine, too," Dana said.

"Really?" he said, tilting his head in surprise.

"You sound surprised," she said with a smile. "But I'm not making it up. My mother really does have an interesting past."

"Was she a policewoman?"

Dana shook her head. "No, nothing like that. But, like your dad, she hung around with some interesting characters."

"Care to elaborate?" he said with a smile.

She didn't, but didn't want to sound rude, then their second order of drinks arrived and she breathed a sigh of relief.

But Tommy wouldn't let it go. He'd shielded himself off from her questions, but wanted to know everything about her.

"Did you become a cop because of your father, or was it your mother's past that made you do it?"

"Yeah, my dad inspired me. You're not going to stop until I tell you about my mother, isn't that right?"

Tommy rested his elbow on the table and rested his face in the palm of his hand. He smiled, that beautiful smile, and nodded.

"But you won't tell me about yours?" she asked.

He nodded again, and she rolled her eyes.

"Maybe I'll tell you someday. Might be soon. Might be a long time. Who knows?" He smiled again, and she could barely sit still. "Tell me about your mother," he said.

"My mother is originally from the city. She and my dad live in the suburbs now."

"And?"

"You really aren't going to stop until I tell you?"

Tommy nodded, watching her with his intense, dark eyes.

"It's not that unusual of a story, but my mother, she had this friend..." Dana paused and got comfortable with revealing the truth to him. It would be okay to tell Tommy because she felt he'd understand. "And this friend of hers, he was a gangster. He was kind of a legend around here. I never met him, but she told me stories about him. He died young."

"What was his name?" Tommy asked.

"Colin, I think, Colin O'Brien," she said, and a look of recognition passed over Tommy's face. "That look," she said with a grin. "What are you hiding?"

"Nothing," Tommy said, but he blushed a little.

"No, tell me," she said, and her hand touched his briefly.

"Maybe some other time," he said. Then he signaled to the bartender and ordered another drink. "Want one?" he asked her.

"Sure," she said, and he ordered her another glass of wine.

Another drink turned into yet another one, and then more for him, and soon they were both drunk.

Dana gradually traced the outline of Tommy's wrist tattoo, a black thorny rose, lightly with her finger.

"You like it?" he asked.

She nodded and giggled, and she couldn't believe she'd giggled. She never did that. But Tommy brought out her feminine side.

"Do you have any tattoos?" he said, and his touch felt hot against her skin as he pushed up her sleeves and searched her arms. "In places I can't see, maybe?" He said faintly and glanced at her breasts through her shirt.

It had been a long time since Dana enjoyed flirting with a man, but she pulled her hand back, suddenly remembering her place as his colleague even in her state of drunkenness.

"I don't have any," she said quietly, looking away from him at a couple seated quietly in the back of the room.

"Hey, I'm sorry," Tommy said, and gave her a tender pat on the shoulder. "I didn't mean to upset you."

"You haven't," she said, looking at him again, but still unwilling to offer more than hints about her attraction to him. "I'm a tough girl, not a delicate flower. I can handle it."

Tommy smiled a little at her, and she wanted to ask him more about his father: Was he a gangster? Had he known Colin? But she didn't want to upset him, so she held back.

"Yeah, but I'm really sorry, Dana," Tommy said, again, with sincerity

"Hey, it's fine, really," she said, patting his hand to assure him, as she felt his remorse was genuine.

"I know we're working together, and I know we don't really know each other that well, but I like you, Dana. I like you a lot."

She wondered how to reply as he held her gaze. Was this him doing the talking, or the drink?

"I like you, too, Tommy," she said after a moment. Then, she took a risk, because she did really like him, and there was a certain vulnerability about him despite his hardened exterior. "What do you say we get out of here?"

"Don't you want another drink?" he said, and she briefly wondered whether he had a problem. He paused then looked at her. "Wait you actually mean it, don't you?"

"Tommy, I'm not asking you if you'd like to sleep with me," she said, and her face felt hot. "I'm asking if you like to leave and eat someplace else. It's too loud in here."

"Oh, that's what you meant," Tommy said, looking at her with a distant gaze and he didn't blush.

Dana detected a touch of disappointment in his voice. "How loose do you think I am, Tommy?" she said with a laugh.

"I wasn't thinking that way," he said, and now he blushed.

"You were," Dana said with a smile. "It's fine."

"Well, maybe a little," he admitted with a shrug.

Tommy signaled to the bartender and asked for the bill.

"I'm not going to let you pay for me," she said.

"Don't worry about it," he replied in a casual way.

"No, Tommy, I mean it. I don't want you to pay for me," she said, putting her hand over his as he set his wallet on the table.

"Why not?" Tommy asked. "We're friends, aren't we?"

"We're colleagues," she said.

"Friends. Colleagues. Still, can't I buy you a drink?"

"All right, you can," she said, reasoning it wouldn't hurt.

"Why do I sense there's a 'but' coming?" he said with a grin.

"That's because there is," she replied. "But I'm buying dinner."

Tommy didn't say anything as he put some money down on the bar for the bill. "I can't let you do that," he said after a while, in a firm tone.

"Are you being serious?" she asked him.

"You don't very much like being told what to do, do you?"

"Well, I'm the boss," she suddenly said, remembering her place and feeling awkward. What the hell was she doing, flirting with him?

"Right, you are," he said, seeming to recall his place as well, and blushing.

They got up and made their way past the tightly packed crowd, still having not decided who would buy dinner.

The street had thickened with people going about their night-time lives, and Tommy and Dana fell into a quiet rhythm as they stood outside the pub, wondering where to go next.

"I'm not hungry anymore," Dana said.

"You mean, you want to go home?"

"Yes, with you," Dana replied, and felt her pulse quicken as she spoke. She reached up and grabbed his shirt collar and he pulled her against the wall outside the pub, out of view from the street.

"Are you sure you want to do this?" he asked her, barely able to keep his hands off her.

She nodded and held onto his belt, pulling him closer to her, and kissing him furiously.

"Where do you live?" she quickly asked him.

"Not nearby," he said, his thinking in line with hers.

"I live a few streets away," she said.

"Let's go to your place, then," he said.

She didn't say anything as she considered what to do, because she knew that agreeing would change their dynamic indefinitely. It wouldn't be something she could just put away and forget.

Then she nodded and grabbed his hand, pulling him down the street as they half ran to her apartment.

"It's this way, not much longer," she kept telling him, and he'd laugh at her enthusiasm.

9

Outside her building, Dana struggled to find her house key in her handbag.

"Damn it, I can't find my key," she said.

Tommy smiled at her then took her bag from her. He went through it carefully until he found her key.

"Here," he said, handing it to her.

"Thanks," she said with a shy smile. She didn't want to seem too eager.

They walked into the hallway, up a set of stairs, and he squeezed her hand as she opened the door to her apartment, then she led him into the living room, where she felt for the light switch on the wall.

Inside her brightened place, he changed and became more assertive, displaying his earlier confidence. He took her by surprise when he lifted her off her feet and set her on the couch. Dana tossed her purse to the floor as he stood over her, watching her in silence, with those intense, dark eyes.

"What?" she said, and laughed a little.

"I'm just thinking how badly I want you," he said, with his voice sounding hoarse from their sprint to her place.

She reached up for him, apprehensive but giving in.

Afterwards, he sat up in her bed with her head on his bare, firm chest, and him stroking her hair. Whether she had made the right decision kept playing over in her mind. His lovemaking hadn't surprised her, but he hadn't been as gentle as she expected.

"What are you thinking?" he asked her, sounding more sober now that time had passed. His hand looked large touching her breast.

"Nothing," she said, not wanting to reveal her doubt. She reached up to his face and traced his scar. "How did that happen?" she asked him, reasoning they knew each other well enough now for her to ask.

"It's a long story," he said.

"Tell me," she said, figuring they had time.

"It's not very interesting."

"I still want to know," she said, with a smile.

"I got into a bad fight when I was younger, in my teens. The other guy had a knife, I didn't. That's what it's like growing up in the city," he said with a smile and a shrug.

"Oh, I'm sorry," she said, because she didn't know what else to say, and because she had grown up in the suburbs, she couldn't really relate. "What happened to the other guy?" she said.

"You don't want to know," he replied.

She laughed then stopped when he made a serious face, and she gave him a shocked look.

"Just kidding," he said with a grin.

Again, she wanted to slap him, and kiss him. That, she could do. She leaned up, and her lips touched his.

He pulled away.

"Tommy, what's wrong?" she asked.

68

"You need to know something about me," he said faintly, and stopped touching her hair.

"What is it?" she asked, and she moved out of his large, hard arms when he didn't reply. "What's going on?" she asked, sensing something wrong. Did he, too, have doubts about what they'd done?

"It's about the case we're working on."

"Oh," she said, somewhat relieved. "What is it?"

Tommy sighed. "If I tell you, it'll change things. Hell, I might not even be working this case anymore, if I tell you."

"Tommy, what is it?" she asked, now worried. She sat up.

"But I don't know if I can keep lying to you," he continued to ruminate to himself.

"What is it?" she asked, feeling the need to grab him and shake him, but not knowing how he'd react. "Tell me!" she finally shouted.

"It's about my mother."

"Oh," Dana said softly. "What does she have to do with our case?"

"My mother's Violet McCarthy."

Dana jumped out of bed and stood looking at him in her underwear in silence for a few moments. "You're joking," she insisted. "But it's not funny."

He looked at her and shook his head.

"But it doesn't make any sense," she said. "They never would have let you worked on the case if they knew."

"No one knows. I haven't told anyone. I took my dad's last name after he died."

"Then why are you telling me?" she asked, because that was the first thing that came to her mind. She couldn't keep a secret like that, because doing so would be against everything she stood for. She was the type of cop who did everything by the book. "We don't know each other that well."

69

"I don't know," Tommy said, seeming surprised himself that he'd told her. "I don't know you well, but for some reason, I felt like I could, like I could trust you. I can, can't I?" Tommy moved over to the side of the bed where she stood.

"You do know what you're asking me to do, don't you? You're asking me to lie to our boss."

"You don't have to lie to him," Tommy said. "He won't ask you about it, because he doesn't suspect anything, so there's no need to tell him anything."

"It will jeopardize our investigation."

"No, it won't."

"Tommy, are you really trying to tell me that you're going to help your own mother get sent to jail?"

A look crossed over his face, as though he hadn't thought of that before.

"I'll do what I have to do. That's part of the job," he finally said, but he didn't sound very convinced.

Dana knew what she had to do as well, but she also knew that telling their boss would mean that Tommy would probably be suspended, or fired, for not disclosing he knew Violet McCarthy, when he'd been assigned to the investigation. She wanted to do the right thing, but she knew that would also be a rotten thing to do to Tommy, whom she cared about.

Her silence seemed to frighten him. "Dana, you can't say anything. Tell me you won't say anything."

"I can't make a decision right now, but I won't say anything for now," she finally said.

She sensed Tommy wouldn't accept an ultimatum, but deep down inside, she felt he would do the right thing and tell their boss, and if he didn't, she knew what she'd have to do.

Tommy nodded, as if he knew her words would have to do for now.

"I feel closer to you now, now that I've told you," he said after a moment, and she sensed that wasn't easy for him to have admitted. "But I need a drink." He gave a slight chuckle. "Do you have anything strong? Whiskey, maybe?"

Dana nodded and left the bedroom for the kitchen, barefoot, feeling unsteady as she walked. If she continued to be with Tommy, what was she getting herself into? Dana had always considered herself a good girl. She wasn't her mother, that was for sure. Her mother had been quite a bad girl, a drinker who'd associated with criminal types, including Colin O'Brien. But Dana's father had helped her mother reform herself, and Dana liked to think of herself as her father's daughter. Tommy wasn't a clear-cut criminal, but he was concealing the truth. Dana never had had a secret as big as covering for Tommy, so that made him exciting to her. Before Tommy, most of the men who'd come in and out of her life over the years, had been, well, pretty boring. With Tommy, she'd have some excitement to look forward to, but for how long could the good girl keep his secret?

In the kitchen Dana opened the cupboard and found the bottle of Irish whiskey that she, ironically, kept there to share a glass with her father sometimes, when he visited with her mother. Tommy had sounded as if he'd wanted the bottle, not just a glass, so she grabbed two glasses and returned to the bedroom. She found Tommy out of bed and dressed, standing by the window, looking outside at the dark city streets dotted with lights. She could hear the sounds of traffic below. He didn't face her when she entered the room. He just stood there, tall and solemn.

"Everything okay?" she asked, then felt foolish for asking. Of course, everything wasn't okay, after what he'd told her. "I have whiskey," she said, when he didn't answer her. "Tommy?"

"Yeah, thanks," he said, turning around to look at her and giving her a warm smile.

Dana handed him the bottle and set the glasses down on her nightstand.

Tommy poured them each a drink and handed Dana hers. He stood looking at her for a moment then smiled.

Dana realized she was just wearing her underwear.

"You're beautiful," he said, with a wink.

"Tommy, I want to ask you something," she said, viewing his compliment as a distraction.

"What is it?" he asked as he finished his glass of whiskey.

Dana had barely sipped hers, but knew it would help take the edge off, so she drank some.

"Are you close to your mother?" she asked quietly.

"Why? Does it make a difference?"

"From the way you talked, I assumed you weren't, but wasn't sure. It's important I know, because, although our boss is in charge of both of us, in a way, I'm also in charge of what happens to you. And I can't accept lies."

"I used to be close to her," he said, then went to pour himself another drink.

Dana sensed he didn't wish to discuss it further, but that he wasn't being entirely honest with her.

"Are you trying to figure out whether I'm working with her behind your back?" Tommy said with a smile, and she couldn't figure out whether he was joking, but she didn't think he was.

"No," Dana replied quickly, not wanting to anger him and escalate the situation.

"Good, because I'm not," he said, and he poured himself another drink.

Dana didn't know him well enough to truly trust him, although she wanted to.

"Maybe you ought to take it easy with the drink," she told him.

"Don't worry about me. I'll be fine," he said, and she saw a darker side of Tommy, one she hadn't seen before.

He trusted her, but she wanted to do the right thing.

"I trust you," he said.

But she felt obligated to tell the truth.

10

C amille awoke to someone pounding on the front door of their house. She turned to Johnny in bed, waking him.

"Who the fuck is that?" Johnny said.

"I have no fucking idea," she replied, but it wasn't Anton again, she was sure of that. She'd only been released from the hospital yesterday.

She checked the time on the alarm clock: 5 in the morning. Who the hell would come to their house so early?

Phoebe spoke outside of their closed bedroom door, "What's going on?" The pretty, dark-haired teenager knocked and came into their room.

"We don't know, sweetie," Camille said to the slender girl.

"It's going to be okay," Johnny said to the both of them. He got out of bed and went to the bedroom window that overlooked the street. "Holy fuck," he muttered under his breath, but Camille heard it. "Camille, there are police cars out there. The police are here."

The first thought that crossed Camille's mind was, what had they done lately that could have warranted their arrival? She could think of many things. She quickly hid their gun in the dresser at the side of the bed.

"What's going on?" Phoebe asked with apprehension thick in her voice.

Camille urgently felt the need to comfort her. "It's okay. Everything's going to be okay, sweetheart," she said, rising from the bed and touching the girl's arm.

Phoebe turned to Johnny, which she often did in times of need, and that was something that really bothered Camille.

"I'm scared, Dad," Phoebe said.

He turned to her and smiled. "Don't worry. Dad's going to make everything all right."

Phoebe didn't know what they were involved in. She just assumed they were business people and had a gun for protection, and Johnny and Camille let her think that because it was better that way. Phoebe was young, and didn't need something that complicated in her life.

"I'll go downstairs and see what they want before they break the fucking door down," he said to Camille, who followed him out of the bedroom. She told Phoebe to wait there.

Camille walked downstairs shadowing Johnny. She tried to think if there was anything besides the gun that they needed to hide before it was too late.

The pounding on the door continued. It had never stopped.

"We're coming!" Johnny shouted when they reached the door. He unlocked and opened it and Detective Highland stood facing them with a mass of police officers standing behind him, all of them staring at the pajama-clad Johnny and Camille.

Oh, fuck. This wasn't good.

"What are you doing here?" Camille asked the detective, pushing her way to the front. She didn't let fear invade her voice. Long ago, she'd made a promise to herself that she would never show fear to the police.

"I'm here to arrest you," Highland replied with a smirk.

"What the fuck are you talking about?" Johnny demanded to the detective. "Camille's the victim here."

"Apparently not," Detective Highland told him.

Phoebe came rushing down the stairs. "Mom? Dad? What's happening?" she asked.

"Stay back, sweetheart," Camille told her, and Phoebe recoiled in fear.

"Are you going to make this easy or hard?" Detective Highland asked Camille as he dangled a pair of handcuffs.

"First, tell me what the fuck this is about. I have rights," she said.

"Yeah, you better tell her," Johnny said to the detective.

"Watch it, honcho," he replied to Johnny.

"Fuck you!" Johnny shouted back at him.

"Are we going to have trouble from you too?" Detective Highland gave Johnny a nasty grin. "Am I going to have to arrest the pair of you in front of your daughter?"

"Leave her out of this, and tell me what the hell is going on," Camille said.

"Violet McCarthy," the detective told her.

"What about her? You arrest her yet?"

"No, we haven't."

"Why the fuck not?" Camille demanded.

"Because you're a damn liar, that's why," the detective said through his teeth.

Camille felt as if all the life had been drained out of her and she went numb. She'd been caught. *Fuck*. She feigned innocence anyway. "I don't understand," she said, glancing from Johnny to the detective, as though in shock.

"We determined that Ms. McCarthy was somewhere else during the time you said she attacked you."

"Maybe it was somebody else who did it. I can't be sure it was her," Camille quickly said.

Detective Highland suppressed a chuckle.

"Save it for someone else. I know all about you, Mrs. Garcia. I looked you up," he replied, as though he'd only recently discovered her criminal ties.

Despite a long life of crime, Camille had never been arrested before, and she feared it.

"Not in front of my daughter," she told the detective in a calm voice.

"You're not taking her anywhere, motherfucker," Johnny said to the detective. The cops standing behind him moved closer, toward Johnny and Camille.

"Am I gonna have to arrest you also?" Highland said to Johnny.

"Johnny, please," Camille said, pleading at him with her eyes. She didn't like giving in to anyone, especially to the police, but she didn't want the situation to get out of hand in front of Phoebe.

"I'll go in peace," she said to the detective. "But you're not putting cuffs on me in front of my kid."

Detective Highland seemed to think for a moment then he nodded. "All right, step outside. We'll do it there."

Which was worse, being arrested in front of her daughter, or her entire suburban neighborhood?

Detective Highland wouldn't let Camille take her cane with her, so she was forced to limp. She braced herself as he took her by the arm and stepped outside into the early morning's strengthening sunlight. When she looked back at Johnny, he seemed to be deciding whether to come to her defense and attack the detective. Camille glanced at Phoebe then at Johnny and shook her head. "Don't," she mouthed to him.

She wondered what she must look like to her neighbors, the few who were up early leaving for work, as she was escorted away from her home by a suited detective and a half a dozen police officers. Then again, the police cars had already shown up a while ago, and although they hadn't used sirens when they arrived, their presence by her driveway was very obvious. So if her neighbors had noticed that something was going on, they already had noticed.

Detective Highland stopped halfway to the cars to handcuff Camille, right in the middle of her front yard. The man across the street, whom she and Johnny would wave to whenever they saw him, was getting into his car and stopped to watch the scene unfold. His mouth hung open in shock.

Camille looked at him and shrugged, because she couldn't wave with her hands behind her back, and what the hell else was she supposed to do?

"Thanks for making me look like an asshole in front of my neighbors," she muttered to Detective Highland.

"It's my pleasure," he replied, his voice heavy with sarcasm.

"Screw you," Camille said, not quietly. She twisted around and spat at him, missing his face by an inch.

"Looking to get an assault charge on top of filing a false report?" he said, no longer smiling.

"Fuck you," Camille said, and he shoved her into the backseat of a police car, with Johnny and Phoebe watching from the doorway. The nerve of the scum, arresting her in front of her family.

"Call Mickey," she shouted to Johnny through the window, but she didn't know if he'd heard her. Regardless, she knew he'd ring Mickey, her stepbrother and her lawyer anyway.

The motorcade of police cars drove off with Detective Highland in the passenger seat and another officer driving, and all of their sirens blaring.

The bastards hadn't even let her get dressed out of her pajamas.

They booked her at the station on charges of filing a false complaint, and then transported her to a local prison while she awaited her chance for a bail hearing.

As Camille stepped off the bus in her new orange jumpsuit, courtesy of the New York Department of Corrections, her stomach tightened, and she disguised her apprehension with a swagger, albeit with a bit of a limp. If the name of the prison sounded familiar to her, that's because it was. It was the same prison where Catherine McCarthy was being held, and Camille and Catherine hated each other almost as much as she and Violet hated one another.

She tripped on a rock in the filth-strewn parking lot and stopped, and the woman behind her, a girl, really, who looked about nineteen years old, bumped into her.

"Watch where you're going, bitch," the girl, a pretty, ginger-haired thing, said when Camille turned around. She gave Camille a menacing glare.

This wasn't her neighborhood, which she controlled, and Camille was outside of her element.

To apologize would look very weak, but to give her silence would create conflict.

Instead, Camille made a joke. "I'm such a clumsy ass," and to her surprise, the girl laughed.

"What they bust you for?" the girl asked her, becoming increasingly more friendly as they walked single file into an entrance, under the command of a muscular female guard.

"Some nonsense. You?" Camille asked.

"Assaulting this bitch I caught with my boyfriend. What's your name?"

"Camille."

"I'm Joy."

"Shut up!" the guard yelled at them as they neared her.

"Bitch," Joy muttered under her breath, and Camille suppressed a giggle.

The guard ordered the line of women to stop, which they all did, some faster than others. She marched straight up to Camille and Joy and came to a halt an inch from their faces. Camille could smell the woman's rancid breath.

"You two think this is funny?" she shouted with sweat glistening on her furrowed brow.

Her expression looked almost comical to Camille, but she didn't dare laugh. So, this guard was evidently the official asshole of the prison. Johnny, who had spent time in prison, had warned her there would be more than one.

Joy smirked at the woman, whose name was Officer Neale, according to the tag on her dull uniform. Officer Neale took her baton and hit Joy across the knees. The young girl howled in pain and fell to the ground, moaning and writhing.

"What about you, you want some, too?" the guard yelled at Camille.

Camille didn't look at her.

"Hey, I'm talking to you!" the guard screamed in Camille's face.

Camille stared at her.

"What about you? Am I going to have a problem with you?"

A surge of bravery rose through Camille. "You shouldn't have hit her," she told the guard, her voice very calm.

Officer Neale laughed in disbelief. Then she smacked Camille across the knees with her baton. Camille flinched, but she didn't fall. Instead, she breathed out her pain.

Officer Neale seemed surprised at Camille's reaction and stared at her in silence. Then she took her club and smacked the back of Camille's legs.

That did it, and Camille couldn't take it any longer. "Fucking bitch," she said under her breath.

"What the hell did you just say to me?" Officer Neale sneered.

"You heard what I said," Camille replied, keeping her gaze on the guard's.

"You're gonna be sorry," the guard replied. She stepped over Joy on the ground and grabbed Camille by the arm. She called for a male guard in the distance, one with a thick mustache, who ran over and grabbed Camille's other arm. Camille considered resisting, but knew they would just beat her more if she did, then she resisted anyway, kicking the dirt and pushing against them, as best she could in her cuffed wrists and shackled ankles, as Officer Neale transferred full control of her to the burly male guard, who proceeded to drag her off the line, away toward the ugly prison building. What did they plan to do with her? To her? Camille didn't know what, but she knew it couldn't be good.

"Hey, thanks," Joy called out to Camille.

She sweated in the heat of the afternoon in the unshaded prison grounds, as she was taken away to a side door on the other side of a gate, which the male guard pushed open with his foot as she elbowed him.

"Little bitch," he whispered. "Stop fucking fighting."

11

I nside of the cool, dark building, another male guard approached. Camille could see the nametag on this one, Bailey.

"We have a new feisty one on our hands," Bailey said to his taller colleague with a sneer. Bailey was on the thinner side, and looked older than his friend.

"What do you want to do with her?" the other guard asked Bailey, who seemed like the superior officer.

"A night in the hole should put her in her place," he replied, still smirking.

The hole—solitary confinement—everyone knew about that dark, lonely place. Even Camille, who had never been imprisoned, knew of its existence from friends on the outside.

"Sounds good," the guard who held her said, then he passed her into Bailey's rough hands.

Camille continued to resist, and Bailey whispered into her ear, his breath warm and foul, "Don't think I won't use the baton on you because you're a woman."

Camille stopped resisting, and watched the other guard walking away into the dark distance. Where was she? In some kind of subterranean section of the prison where the hole was located?

"Are you gonna behave now?" Bailey asked.

Though she doubted he'd go easy on her either way, she looked straight at him and nodded.

"Good, but that doesn't mean you'll get to spend the night upstairs," he said, grabbing her by the handcuffs and pulling her down the hallway, which was lit by a single ceiling light.

"Where are we going?" she asked to calm herself, though she already knew.

"*You're* going," he snapped at her. "Where do you think?" He smirked.

"I don't give a shit," she said.

"Sure, you don't."

They stopped in front of a tall metal door among other metal doors. Camille could hear someone coughing and someone else weeping faintly. Other prisoners.

"You'll have plenty of company," Bailey said with a chuckle, as he opened the door with one of his keys.

"I won't be in here long," Camille told him in defiance, as he opened the door and shoved her inside. "My husband will make sure I get bail."

Bailey laughed to himself. "Keep telling yourself that."

He removed Camille's handcuffs, but left her legs shackled, making it difficult for her to navigate in her prison-issued sandals. She smacked the door as Bailey shut it in her face.

"Take these fucking things off my legs," she yelled.

"Bye, bye," he sang as he locked the door. He whistled as he walked away.

With the door shut, darkness fell in the room. Total darkness. Camille couldn't even see her hands as she held them out in front of her. A tiny sliver of light came in through a slat in the door, which Camille assumed was so the guards could pass food and water to her. She hadn't seen a bed in the room before the door closed, just a floor, which felt hard and cold as she sat on it. She struggled to maneuver with her legs shackled, but managed to lean against the wall. Something small and smooth began to crawl against her bare arm and she quickly pulled away. Whatever it was, she heard it scurry across the floor. Must have been an insect, perhaps a cockroach. She willed herself not to scream, but wouldn't let Bailey hear her suffering. Not even a nasty bug could propel her to do that. Alone in the dark room, she could hear herself breathing, and the sounds of the other women in the rooms next to her, crying and coughing. She started to talk to the women. What else could she do with her time?

"Hello?" she called out in the darkness. She somewhat anticipated Bailey would overhear and yell at her to shut up.

"Hey," a woman replied. "You're new here?" She sounded older.

"Yeah. How did you know?" Camille asked.

"From the way you talked back to the guard, that Bailey asshole," she said quietly, as if she didn't want him to hear them.

"What's the deal with him, anyway?"

"He's bad, but not the worst. You scared?"

Camille wasn't sure whether the question was genuine or a taunt. "No, I can handle it," she spoke with confidence. "What's your name?" she asked, having decided to ignore her earlier doubt. She wanted to have someone to talk with.

"Esther. Yours?"

"Camille."

"Nice to meet you. Wish it were better circumstances," she said with a slight laugh.

Camille smiled, but knew Esther couldn't see her. "Who's the other girl down here with us?"

"Don't know her name. She sounds like she's just a kid."

"Was she the one who was crying?" Camille asked. The sound seemed to have dissipated.

"Yeah. Sounds like she's just a kid," Esther repeated.

Camille thought of Joy and wondered what was happening up above them.

"So, why they put you here? You talked back or what?" Esther asked her.

"Yeah, to this one named Neale, a woman. She was beating on this girl, who was new like me."

"Neale's a real bitch. Watch out for her, she's the worst of them all."

"Thanks. I'll be careful."

Once again, the sound of the crying girl filled the room.

"Hey, you okay?" Esther asked her.

The girl didn't answer and continued to cry.

"Guess she don't want to talk," Esther said to Camille.

"Hey," Camille said, trying to talk to the girl. "Are you all right?"

"No," the girl finally replied, her voice heavy with emotion. "I shouldn't even be in this awful place."

"Down here or just in jail in general?" Camille asked.

"In jail. They say I assaulted my boyfriend, but he was the one who was beating on me, so I stopped him. What you girls in here for?" she asked.

"Knifed this bitch," Esther said. "Knifed this bitch who was bothering my cellmate."

"Oh," Camille said, not really surprised. "She dead?"

"Nah," Esther said with a chuckle. "Probably in the hospital or some shit."

"What are your names?" the girl asked them.

"Esther."

"Camille."

"Camille O'Brien?" the girl said.

"Yeah, but nobody's called me that in a long time, not after I married my husband, Johnny."

"You two know each other?" Esther asked them.

"No, but I grew up in her neighborhood." There was a pause amongst the women. "How about you, Camille, what did you do?" the girl asked, seeming uncertain, given Camille's position of power. "I'm Stephanie, by the way."

"You're not going to believe it," Camille said, wondering how much to disclose. "But I had my mother beat the shit out of me, to make it look like someone I hate did it to me. Obviously, I didn't get away with it," she said with a laugh.

"Why you hate her?" Esther asked.

"It's a long story, goes back years," Camille said.

"I think I know who you're talking about," Stephanie said.

"I don't. Anyway, we got plenty of time to listen," Esther said.

So, she told them the story.

"It goes back to my father. I never knew him. He was murdered by the grandfather of this woman named Violet. The grandfather was a gangster like my father. My father was betrayed by him."

"I know of her. I know about Violet," Stephanie said. "Seen her around the neighborhood. Never talked to her."

"This all happened before you were born, or too young to remember," Camille said. "But maybe you've heard the stories."

"Anyway, after Violet's grandfather died, she and her mother inherited control of the grandfather's side of things. We're all Irish. When I found out what they'd done to my father, I decided I wanted what they had. My Dad would have been in control of our neighborhood's Irish section if it wasn't for that bastard family. And I got control. Then I found out that bitch is dealing in my neighborhood."

"What's her mother's name again? What's Violet's mother's name?" Stephanie asked.

"Catherine," Camille said.

"Catherine McCarthy?" Esther asked, her voice full of surprise.

"Yeah."

"She's in here. She's nasty. I'd be careful if I were you. Her and her crew got a mean reputation."

"I know."

"What you gonna do about her?" Esther asked, though not in a challenging way.

"Haven't figured that out yet," Camille said. "I'll think of something."

"Let me know if you need help," Esther said.

Camille wondered whether the offer was genuine. "You hardly know me," she said.

"I know, but I like you."

"Yeah, me, too, I'll help," Stephanie said, although she didn't sound very sure.

Footfall sounded in the hallway and Camille could hear whistling. Bailey.

"Hello, ladies," Neale said, outside her door, surprising her. "I'm going to have to ask you to shut the fuck up. There's no talking down here. You know the rules, Esther," she said loudly. "Esther, you've been down here many times before."

"Sorry, Officer Neale," Esther said, as though she feared the guard's wrath.

And Camille imagined that Neale was someone to fear, if she frightened the likes of a tough woman like Esther.

"What did you say, Esther? Say it louder, because I can't hear you!" Neale shouted.

"I'm sorry, Officer Neale."

"I'm waiting, Stephanie," Neale yelled at the girl.

"I'm sorry, Ms. Neale," the girl replied, her voice sounding fragile.

"That's officer to you," Neale snapped at her.

"Yes, Officer Neale."

"How about you, new girl, Camille Garcia, or whatever the hell your name is?" Neale said.

Camille didn't want to apologize to this bitch. It went against every bone she had in her body. But she knew that if she didn't, she'd be spending another night down there in the dark.

"Yeah, sorry," she mumbled.

"Come again?"

"I said, sorry," Camille replied with more volume.

Neale tapped her baton against Camille's door. "That's much better, Garcia. Say, is that your married name? Now that I think of it, you don't look Spanish."

Camille didn't wish to discuss her personal life with this woman, but she also knew that Neale expected an answer from her.

"I'm married," she said.

"Garcia, that's your husband's name?" Neale asked.

"It is."

Camille braced herself for a cruel remark about Johnny's heritage.

"That's very interesting," Neale replied.

Camille wanted to retort and ask her just what she meant by that remark, but she held herself back. Sure, another night in solitary would mean that she wouldn't have to face Catherine McCarthy just yet, but Camille wasn't one to avoid a challenge.

Luckily, Neale dropped the subject and continued walking down the corridor.

"When are we gonna eat?" Esther called out to her.

"When I want you to," Neale sang back.

Esther sighed. "We're supposed to get two hot meals down here, and we didn't even get one yet today."

"How long have you been down here?" Camille asked her,

her body filling with dread, with fear of being left in the dark, confined, unfurnished space without windows for more than a day.

"It's been days," Esther replied. "Days."

"I thought they couldn't put you down here for more than twenty-four hours. I thought those are the rules."

Esther breathed out, like she couldn't believe Camille's naivety. "There are no rules in this place. The guards set the rules, and they do what they please."

"Stephanie, how long have you been down here?" Camille asked the girl as panic began to set it. She stood up and paced back and forth in the dark, her hands colliding with the wall each time.

"Since yesterday," Stephanie answered. "They were supposed to let me out this morning, but never did."

"You getting scared?" Esther asked Camille, in a neutral way.

"No," Camille said. "Just not used to this shit." She figured that at least she hadn't been crying like Stephanie.

"Don't worry, you will be soon," Esther said.

The women quieted as the hours wore on, and eventually Camille became tired, but she didn't want to drift off the sleep on the floor, which she suspected was dirty although she couldn't see it, so she stood, leaning against the wall, and closed her eyes. Just for a moment, she told herself. Just a few moments.

She awoke to the sound of something being pushed through the slat in the door, as light filtered in.

She heard Neale's voice say, "Meal-time, princess."

Camille grabbed the tray and Neale closed the slat.

She couldn't see the food in front of her, but when she poked at it with her fingers, it felt cold, thick, and wet.

"I know what you're thinking," Esther's voice said. "That it's shit. It is, but you better eat it. You don't know when you'll get another chance to eat."

Camille suddenly felt dirty. It was everything at once, the vile floor, the disgusting food which she didn't want to eat any more than she wanted to be imprisoned, and this cold, dark place.

She sat down and ate.

12

At what felt like the next morning, but could have been later, Camille's cell door opened and Neale entered.

"Time to go, princess," Neale said with a wicked grin.

"What about the others?" Camille asked, concerned for them.

"They already left, hours ago. You must have been sleeping."

Camille hadn't heard the other cell doors opening, and she had no reason to trust Neale, but she had fallen asleep sometime during the night.

Neale put handcuffs on her then ordered her to move. Camille stepped out into the hallway after Neale.

"What happened to your face?" Neale asked her.

Camille shrugged, and Neale laughed.

"Eyes on the floor," Neale ordered and motioned for Camille to walk ahead of her.

Camille scowled to herself then followed the order.

"What's with the limp?" Neale asked her. "I noticed it before."

None of your fucking business, Camille thought.

"Garcia, I asked you a question," Neale said. "Answer me."

"It's from an old injury," Camille muttered, then she thought she heard Neale chuckle softly to herself. Bitch.

Neale ordered her to stop when they came to a door, and reached around Camille and unlocked it. Then she stepped to the front, opened the door, and demanded that Camille follow her outside.

From being in the total darkness overnight, the daylight hurt Camille's eyes. She trailed Officer Neale across the large courtyard, with the sun warming her cold skin, where a few women were playing basketball, and others stood in groups chatting. She followed Neale inside the prison, past what looked like an empty cafeteria, and up a large set of stairs, shuffling along in her shackled legs. She'd wondered whether she'd see Esther and Stephanie again, the prison was such a vast, complex place.

They entered a giant area with multiple floors that held the women's cells. Many of the women stared at Camille from behind bars as she walked past them, and a few hollered at her and some whistled.

"Hey, baby, we heard you been bad," a young woman with beautifully braided hair said to her with a smile and a laugh.

"Yeah, she been bad," another replied.

Not in the mood for a fight, Camille ignored the women.

"Oh, don't let them get to you," an older woman with a grandmotherly appearance, added.

Camille glanced at her and gave her a nod.

"Move it, Garcia," Neale yelled over her shoulder, when she saw that Camille was trailing behind her.

Camille begrudgingly quickened her pace, and Neale led her up one of the huge metal staircases to the second level. Camille looked up and saw that there was another level above them. A high railing kept the women and guards from tumbling out below as they walked to the cells alongside it. Neale stopped at the fourth cell and turned to stare at Camille.

"Welcome home," she said with one of the nasty grins Camille had come to know well over the brief time they'd been acquainted.

To her surprise, Joy sat on one of the beds in the cell. The girl smiled and waved at her.

"I believe you two already know each other," Officer Neale said to them.

She opened the cell and gave Camille a shove inside then undid her handcuffs and leg shackles. Camille scowled at the guard as she shut the cell and walked away.

"Have fun," she sang out as she left the area.

"She's such a fucking bitch," Joy said to Camille.

"She really is," Camille replied, as she sat down on the bed opposite Joy.

"Thanks for earlier," Joy told her.

"You're welcome," Camille said, looking around the bare cell, her temporary home.

"Was the punishment bad?" Joy asked her.

"Nothing I couldn't handle," Camille said, not wanting to reveal the truth. "How are the other women here?" she asked to change the subject.

"There are some assholes, but most are decent. There's one who's a total bitch, though. She's pretty much in charge of the whole place."

"What's her name?" Camille asked, though she felt she already knew the answer.

"McCarthy. Catherine. Call her Cathy at your own risk," Joy said quietly, as if she feared Catherine overhearing her.

Camille wondered how much about her past dealings with Catherine she should reveal to Joy.

Joy picked up on her hesitation. "Do you know her or something?" she asked. "You got so quiet just now."

"Yeah, you could say I know her."

"How? If you don't mind my asking."

Camille minded, but she didn't want to get off to a bad start with her new cellmate.

"McCarthy is from the same neighborhood as me," she told Joy. "Her and her daughter and me, we go way back."

"They're your friends?" Joy asked, and the question made her seem more innocent than she probably was.

"No," Camille said with a slight laugh. "Them and I, we're definitely not friends."

"Oh, I'm sorry; I didn't mean to pry."

"It's fine, no worries," Camille said. She noticed there was a book on Joy's bed, which she hadn't seen when she first entered the cell. "What are you reading?" she asked, to let the girl know everything really was fine between them.

"A crime novel I found in the library. They let us go in there earlier."

"Is it any good?"

"A bit. Do you like to read?"

"Sometimes," Camille replied.

"Your face, how did you get injured? I noticed it earlier," Joy said to her.

"Long story. It's how I ended up in here. Turns out, it wasn't a good idea. Maybe I'll tell you someday."

"How come you got a limp?"

"I was shot," Camille replied.

"When?"

"Years ago." She paused. "This Catherine you mentioned," she said. "Does she have a big crew in here?"

"Oh, yeah. They run the place along with the guards from what I heard. You meet any of the other girls yet?"

"There were two others down in solitary with me."

"Do you know their names?"

"Yeah. Esther and Stephanie." Camille sat down on her bed.

"Stephanie? If it's the same Stephanie I met, then she's part of Catherine's crew."

"No, she can't be," Camille said, musing to herself. The girl had seemed so innocent.

"I'd be careful if I were you. I heard that Stephanie likes to play games. I would assume she knows who you are."

"I can take care of myself," Camille spoke with confidence, "but thanks."

"One thing's clear to me," Joy said, "We're gonna need our own crew in here if we want to survive. Who else do you know in here?"

Camille thought of saying Esther, but because she had an independent personality, she said, "Thanks, but I won't be in here long enough to need that. I'm confident I'll make bail."

"Suit yourself," Joy said without sarcasm. "Let me know if you change your mind. I know a couple other women in here, and I'm sure we can form our own crew."

Camille had dinner in the cafeteria with Joy and her friends later that day. She spotted Esther and waved, but didn't see Catherine or Stephanie. The next morning the women were permitted to use the bathroom to shower. Camille hadn't bathed in days and felt like shit, so she looked forward to a hot shower, even if it was in a group setting. She walked into the room with Joy and her friends, but they all finished before her and exited, and Camille found herself alone in the bathroom, drying herself off.

She heard a noise, and at the other side of the foggy shower room, she saw someone standing there in prison sandals and an orange jumpsuit, their face obscured by the mist.

"What the fuck?" Camille muttered to herself as she wrapped the towel around her body. "Who the hell is there?"

She heard someone entering and saw two more sets of feet standing alongside the taller woman.

"I'm not playing games," Camille shouted. "Who the fuck is there?"

The tall woman stepped out from the fog, and immediately Camille recognized her. Catherine McCarthy, although older and slightly more haggard than when Camille had last seen her years ago, was unmistakable and still very attractive, her beautiful dark hair, now streaked with white.

"You girls know about this bitch," Catherine said, in her husky voice. "This is the bitch who stole the neighborhood from me and my girl, Violet."

The other women standing at her sides stepped forward. Both were younger than Catherine. One of them, an attractive blonde older than the other, laughed.

"She don't look like much," she said to the other two.

The youngest of the three, a petite brunette, replied, "She sure don't," with a sneer directed at Camille, who recognized the voice as Stephanie's.

Joy's warning had been correct.

Camille stood with the raggedy towel wrapped around her body and moved into a fighting stance.

"Three against one, that's hardly fair," she said to Catherine. "Afraid to come on your own?"

"If you're implying something about my age, you can go fuck yourself," Catherine spat out at her. "I couldn't believe when I heard you got put in here. At first, I couldn't believe my luck. Then I wasn't sure. Now, I know it's really you. I had to come see for myself."

Three against one. Camille knew she was fucked, that she couldn't win. She was a good fighter, but she had no weapons on her, no equalizers, and Catherine and her crew might have them. She searched the outlines of their bodies for a sign of a weapon and saw what looked like a shank in Catherine's hand.

Catherine noticed her looking and said with a smile, "I'm going to watch you bleed out, Camille. I'm going to make you pay for everything you've done to my family."

"I only did it because of what you did to mine," Camille said calmly. "If you hadn't helped kill my father, then I wouldn't have done anything to you and your daughter."

"It is what it is," Catherine said, as Camille formulated a plan to deflect them. Catherine clearly wasn't open to negotiation. Camille searched the area for an exit, but they were blocking the sole one. Fuck it. She wasn't going to let anyone back her into a corner. She'd fight, and if she died trying, then at least she would have gone out brave. She just hoped Johnny and Phoebe would understand if it came to that.

"I'm not going to back down, Cathy," she said, using the name she had once spoken with affection when she'd worked for Catherine and Violet and had been friendly with them.

"I wouldn't expect you to," Catherine replied.

"You'll have to kill me," Camille said.

"I'm well aware of that."

Camille didn't believe she could count on a guard to come to her rescue, as Joy had made it clear that Catherine was in cahoots with the guards. She must have been set up. By whom? Neale? Joy?

"You're gonna cut me?" Camille said to Catherine. "What a coward you are. Why not fight me one on one? Come on, Cathy, let's have a go, just the two of us, and let the girls watch at the sidelines."

"I'll pass," Catherine quipped.

"Afraid you'll lose?"

Catherine stared at her in silence for a second then cleared her throat. "Goodbye, Camille," she said and lunged toward her.

Camille jumped out of her way, but couldn't escape on either side of her, as Stephanie and the other woman blocked her path. She looked for a quick escape, and her only option was to push one of the other women out of the way and make a run for it.

Catherine came at her again, Camille darted around her, and went straight toward Stephanie, reasoning she'd be easier to get past than the other one.

Stephanie ran toward her and tried to punch her in the face, but Camille ducked, and the girl missed. Stephanie came at her again and hit Camille in the jaw. The girl wasn't as feeble as she'd assumed. Camille flew backwards, but caught herself against the wall before she could land on the ground. Catherine turned around and came at Camille as she steadied herself, with the glistening shank in Catherine's hand, pointed directly at her. Fuck, that thing looked sharp. Camille tried to move around Catherine, and out of her reach, but the other woman, the blonde, stood in her way with her arms crossed, shaking her head.

"You're not going anywhere, sweetie," she said with a little smile on what Camille noticed was her strikingly attractive face.

S tephanie came at her from behind, followed by Catherine, and the two women grabbed Camille by the arms. She kicked her legs in the air, trying to push the blonde off her. Catherine tossed the shank to the blonde woman, who held it at the very edge of Camille's chin, taunting her.

"Still letting others do your dirty work for you?" Camille sneered at Catherine. "What's the matter, Cathy," she said, as Catherine flinched slightly, "can't do the deed yourself?" Camille breathed heavily as she struggled to break free.

"Shut up, you fucking bitch," Catherine said. "Cut her, Sharon. Slice this fucking bitch's throat and do it fast," she ordered the blonde woman.

Camille noticed a flicker of hesitation cross the woman's face and figured she could use it to her advantage. She swung her legs at Sharon's stomach, and the woman fell back onto the floor. The shank flew across the room and landed at the other side of them.

Stephanie, who seemed less experienced, released Camille's arm, and Camille wriggled out of Catherine's grasp, who couldn't control her by herself. Camille hobbled out of the shower room and ran straight into the guard Neale outside.

From the satisfied, smug look on her face, Camille just knew that she had something to do with what just happened, but she couldn't just go and accuse a guard. Neale had had it in for her from the very beginning.

"Have a nice shower, Garcia?" Neale said with a sinister grin on her round face.

Knowing sarcasm wouldn't get her anywhere except something bad with the guard, Camille answered her, "It was fine."

Neale looked at her for a moment, as if deciding whether she liked the answer, then said, "Go on. Hurry back to your cell. Be careful," she added, "It can be dangerous around here."

Camille wanted to tell the guard to go fuck herself, but at the same time, she knew that would only get her another night in solitary, so she trudged away with her head held high.

Halfway, a male guard she hadn't seen before collected her and escorted her the remainder of the way to her cell. He opened her cell and let her inside, where Joy waited, looking out the pathetic excuse for a window, a small square that looked out onto the courtyard.

If she had been set up, it might have been Neale, or it could have been Joy. Camille waited until the guard shut the cell to remark to Joy, "You'll never guess what just happened to me in the shower room."

Joy turned around to look at her, and her expression wasn't exactly a worried one, but it wasn't entirely placid either.

"What?" the girl said.

"I almost got shanked by Catherine McCarthy and her friends."

Joy shook her head, as though she thought that was terrible. "They didn't hurt you, though, so that's good."

"No, they didn't. There were three of them, but I'm not that easy to hurt. The thing is somebody must've set me up. Some people, that is, must've helped it happen."

"What are you saying?" Joy said with a grimace. "Are you saying I had something to do with it?"

"Did you? You and your friends all left me in there, and then Catherine and her crew appeared."

"Maybe it was one of the guards," Joy offered.

"Yeah, one of them probably helped, too. But, why did you all disappear suddenly?"

"Because we were done," Joy said. "You sound fucking paranoid."

"I'm learning you have to be in here." Camille wondered if she'd been wrong to accuse the girl, but she had to watch her back, especially inside these walls.

Joy sat on her bed and pretended to look at her fingernails.

"Thinking of getting a manicure?" Camille asked in jest, feeling a little bad that she'd accused the girl, when she didn't have any evidence.

"I probably won't be getting one of those for a long time," Joy replied with a slight smile, and Camille knew that everything was good between them.

"You were right about Stephanie," Camille said to Joy. "She's part of Catherine's crew."

"Yeah, I heard she's a sneaky one." Joy paused then asked her, "What are you gonna do about them trying to slice you? You know they're gonna come after you again."

"I know," Camille said. "I'm hoping to be out of here on bail before they can." She was due for a visit from Johnny tomorrow, and she hadn't seen him in what felt like a month but were merely days.

❧

The next day, Camille was escorted into the visiting room, and a guard told her to sit at one of the small orange tables. She spotted Neale standing at the other side of the room, watching her. She gave Camille a sardonic smile, and Camille just stared at her. She kept her head turned to the doorway as she waited for Johnny to enter the room.

After a few minutes, he came in along with a group of other visitors with a guard Camille didn't recognize leading them. Another guard brought Johnny to her table, and he sat down across from her. Seeing Johnny's handsome face across from her filled her with a longing to escape. She could feel Neale watching them, and looked up across the room, and, indeed, she was.

Johnny reached across the table to stroke her hand, and a male guard shouted, "No touching!"

Johnny pulled away with a despondent expression.

Camille had so many things she wanted to ask him, starting with how were he and Phoebe coping to had he heard from her lawyer? She hadn't received a visit from him yet and wondered what was going on.

"How are you?" Johnny asked her before she could begin her questions.

"I've been better," Camille said with a slight laugh. "It's so good to see your face."

"Are you doing okay in here? I've served time. I know how hard it can be. How are you finding it?" he asked, as though he dreaded to hear her answer.

Camille didn't want to alarm him too soon by revealing what had happened to her in the shower room. She planned to let it slip out gradually.

"It's what I expected," she said with honesty.

"How are the other women treating you? I would imagine it's

better with women than from what I remember from my time with the guys in the slammer."

"The girls can be just as bad," she said, "if not worse."

Johnny's brow crinkled in concern. "Is there something going on, Camille?" he asked.

She'd never been able to fool him in the past so why had she thought she'd be able to now? She didn't want to frighten him, but she couldn't lie to him. Johnny was one of the few people she trusted with all her heart.

"Catherine McCarthy, remember her?" Camille said.

"Yeah. What about her?" Johnny asked, his brow furrowing even more.

"She's in here with me."

"What? How is that possible?"

"It just is."

"We've got to get you out of here," Johnny said, pursing his lips, and his mind seemed to be racing for ideas.

"She came after me in the bathroom, her and some of her friends," Camille said.

"Did they hurt you?"

Camille shook her head.

"We've got to do something about this," Johnny said.

She sat there, looking at him, the reality numbing her.

"Camille, this is serious," he said when she didn't respond.

"They didn't hurt me. I got away," she said.

"Yeah, but they're gonna come after you again. They're gonna keep coming after you until they get you. You know how it works."

"What has Mickey said to you? He hasn't visited me in here yet."

"I talked to him. He's trying to get you out of here, but the prosecutor is a real asshole. The bitch's got it in for us. She's giving Mickey a hard time, and the judge is falling for it."

"It's probably that detective, the one who arrested me," she said. "He seemed like a real fucker."

"No, it's the judge. His father was the judge for your father's trial. I think he's got it in for you."

Her father, Colin, had been convicted of murdering his abusive step-father as a teenager, and had served many years in prison. He'd joined a gang upon his release.

"Are you fucking kidding me?" Camille said, then realized she'd raised her voice, so she said quietly, "I've got bad luck, don't I?" She could've laughed, really, as she couldn't believe her shit luck. "What the hell has he got against me?"

Johnny shrugged. "Maybe he thinks the apple doesn't fall far from the tree." Johnny gave her a wink. "I'm gonna think of something, so don't you worry. I'm gonna work on getting you out of here, baby. Mickey and me, we're gonna get you out of here."

"You better do it fast, Johnny. I think Catherine's got some of the guards on her side in here. She's got help."

"Which ones?" Johnny asked, peering around the room.

"That one over there across the room, that bitch," Camille said, indicating Neale without pointing her out to Johnny.

"She sure looks like a mean bitch," Johnny said.

"That's because she is one," Camille said with a smile. She paused. "How's Phoebe handling everything? And you? How are you, really?"

"Phoebe's worried about you. She's never known anyone who's gone to jail before, except for me."

Camille knew she was a mother figure to the teenage girl, and didn't want to set a bad example.

"Tell her not to be like me," she told Johnny and gave him a serious look. "Tell her she's got to finish school and maybe go to a university."

Camille wanted a proper life for her stepdaughter, and didn't want her becoming involved in gangs like had been her family's history.

"I'll tell her," Johnny said to her with a wistful smile. "But you're a good woman, Camille, and I'd love for her to turn out like you. I really want to kiss you right now."

"Don't," she said, not wanting to concern him further by mentioning her time in solitary confinement, but not wanting to spend another night down there either.

Johnny gave her a look, like he understood her reason without her having to explain.

"I love you," he said.

"I love you, too," she replied, not wanting him to leave, but knowing he couldn't stay.

14

Johnny had never loved anyone more than he loved Camille, and he would do absolutely anything to get her bailed from prison. Anything. Money was not an issue, not these days. Although, at one time, it very much had been.

As soon as he left the prison grounds, he drove to Mickey's offices in the city, stopping at a gas station on the way there to ring Mickey and let him know he would be arriving shortly.

In the city he parked near the law offices, and entered the building, past the security guard, who knew him, and toward the elevators. Upstairs in the office, he said hello to Mickey's voluptuous secretary, who rang Mickey in his office.

A moment later, a door opened, and Mickey, a short, handsome, muscular man with light hair, in a slick dark suit and red tie with shiny black shoes, stepped out with his arms extended to embrace Johnny.

"Johnny," the ever-affectionate Mickey said. "How are you doing? I know you've been better," he said, answering his own question. "And my stepsister? How is she? You've been to see her? I was just getting around to visiting her myself this afternoon."

"She's not doing well, Mickey. She's got an enemy on the inside, and they're after her. They attacked her. I think they'll kill her if they can. At the very least, she's gotta be moved to a different jail."

Mickey shook his head in astonishment. "That's terrible, Johnny. Listen, we're going to get her out of there, out of jail completely, don't you worry," he spoke with confidence.

"But how? You said so yourself; the judge is a fucking asshole."

Mickey glanced at his secretary. "Let's step into my office," he said, and touched Johnny's arm lightly.

Johnny followed him inside, and Mickey shut the door.

"Have a seat," Mickey said, pointing to one of the comfortable-looking chairs in front of the desk.

Johnny sat and folded his hands in his lap while he waited for Mickey to sit down.

"How's Phoebe?" Mickey asked, as he sat across from Johnny, with his hands on the gleaming, immense wooden desk.

"She's confused. She's always thought so highly of Camille, you know, and now she doesn't understand what's going on."

"Have you explained it to her?"

"We try to keep her out of our lifestyle because we think that's best, for her not to be involved. She knows Camille was hurt by somebody, obviously, but she's too old for me to lie to her, so I've just told her someone made a false accusation."

"I'd be careful what you say to her," Mickey replied. "I wouldn't put it past these pricks to try to get your own daughter to testify against Camille." He paused. "Anyway, the most important thing now is that we get her the hell out of that place."

"What's your plan?" Johnny asked, his voice filled with eagerness.

"The judge who's not giving her bail, the thing about his

father's connection to Camille, I think I can get a new judge on the case. I've filed the paperwork needed to do so. I'm claiming his father's connection to Camille makes him biased."

"Then you're going to, what, bribe the new judge?" Johnny asked, unsure about the idea.

"No, that'd be too risky. There's a good chance that the new judge will give her bail. I think this guy just has it in for her because of their fathers' history. I really believe a new judge will be in her favor."

"How long is this going to take?" Johnny asked.

"Shouldn't be more than a day or two. You think she can last that long?"

"Catherine McCarthy, the woman who's after her on the inside, is a fucking mean bitch, but my Camille, she's very strong."

A few days later, Camille stood outside of the prison's high gates awaiting Johnny's arrival in the cool morning air on a cloud-filled day. He'd gotten her out of there like he promised he would.

She had barely said goodbye to Joy, whom she still wondered if she could trust, and she had never seen Esther again. But Neale had been there to see her off, and she'd told Camille she was "lucky". Camille wondered what that meant. Lucky to have not been killed by Catherine and her gang? She'd avoided that by never again being alone, and she hadn't showered in all that time. Or had Neale meant, lucky to have escaped her? One thing was for sure, Camille never wanted to return to that prison again, and would do anything to ensure that didn't happen.

A few minutes later, Johnny arrived in one of their less flashy cars. Probably best, in case that detective was watching them from somewhere nearby.

Johnny parked alongside her and exited with his arms opened widely to embrace her. She'd left the prison in the clothes she'd arrived in.

"How's my girl?" he asked with a smile, his eyes shining with affection.

"I knew I could count on you," she told him as she held onto his warm, strong body. "How did you manage to do it?"

"It was mostly Mickey's doing, but I hurried him along. He got a new judge to oversee your bail because of the other judge's connection to your dad, and this guy was softer than the other one. And here we are." Johnny smiled again, and Camille kissed him with passion.

"I wondered if Phoebe would come here with you," Camille said.

"I asked her if she wanted to, but I think she was a little scared. I'm sure she'll be okay once you're home. Your mother's already there; she's waiting with her."

Camille nodded, but inside she hoped their relationship wouldn't be different.

"How's my mother doing?" Camille asked.

She had rung Sheila a few times from the prison, but her mother hadn't visited her. It hadn't upset her, though, because she knew her mother didn't like prisons because of Camille's father, and Camille respected her mother's wishes.

"She's doing good. Ready to go home?" Johnny asked her as he opened the passenger side door for her.

"Hell, yeah, I'm ready," Camille said with a genuine smile, but once inside the car, her heart sank a little with the reality of having to face a temperamental teenager at home. She and her stepdaughter were close, but they had drifted apart because the older Phoebe became, the more she seemed to miss her late mother.

A few hours later, they arrived home, and Camille had somewhat anticipated seeing the media or their neighbors queued up to watch her, but the street was mostly empty despite it being a weekend.

Sheila ran out of the house as soon as Johnny parked in the driveway.

"Darling," she said to Camille as she wrapped her up in a tight embrace. "I knew they'd never really be able to hurt you in there," she said. She had told her mother about Catherine's gang on the phone.

"Never," Camille said.

"That's my tough girl," Sheila said, patting her back tenderly.

"Where's Phoebe?" Camille asked eagerly. She had expected the girl to greet her outside.

"She's in her room," Sheila said, touching Camille's hand, knowing Camille's concern because she was a mother herself.

Then Camille wanted to run upstairs and yell at the girl, scream at her for being so selfish when her mother had just come home. They'd always had a good relationship, even before Camille's marriage to Johnny, but, now, something seemed to have changed between them, and Camille hoped she could fix whatever that was.

Camille hadn't brought any belongings to the prison and she didn't have anything to take home with her, so Johnny just closed the car doors and they went inside the large, beautiful white house. Johnny had mentioned that the police had gotten a search warrant to search the house after they arrested her, but that he'd stashed their guns at a safe house in the city.

The day had gotten hotter, and inside the air conditioning felt like a relief to Camille's skin. The prison had been so unbearably warm most of the times, and a lot of other things had been unbearable as well, but Camille had made it out alive and well.

"Do you want a glass of wine?" Sheila asked, despite the early hour, for she knew her daughter well.

"No, thanks, I'll wait," Camille said and went straight upstairs to Phoebe's room. Johnny followed but she motioned that she wanted to do it alone.

"I'll go downstairs and take your mother up on that drink," he said with a smile.

15

In the hallway, Camille found Phoebe's door closed, and rather than open it outright, she knocked lightly.

"Who is it?" Phoebe said, although she must have known who it was. Her bedroom window overlooked the driveway.

"Phoebe, you know who it is," Camille said, slightly exasperated. She turned the doorknob but found it locked. "Don't be like this. Open the door," she said, twisting the knob frantically. Part of her wanted to kick the door down, and the other part of her wanted to cry. Instead, she said, "You're being selfish, Phoebe. I haven't seen you in almost a week."

Camille heard movement behind the door, and after a moment, it opened slowly. Phoebe stood there at the other end, looking at her.

Camille smiled. "How's it going, gorgeous?" she said to the pretty teenager.

Phoebe shrugged without a smile. "How come you were sent to jail?" she asked.

"Can I come in?" Camille asked, gesturing to the door.

Phoebe nodded, and Camille entered and sat on her stepdaughter's bed.

"It was a misunderstanding," she told her.

Phoebe gave her a doubtful look. "Grandma wouldn't say when I asked her, but I know that isn't the truth. You can't hide it from me forever. Someday I'll find out."

Camille recalled back to the conversation she'd had with her own mother, when she was young, about her father being a gangster, and considered how much she should reveal to Phoebe, how much could she handle at once? It was true Phoebe would eventually grow up and discover who and what her parents were. She and Johnny had decided they would protect her for as long as they could, but that someday they'd have to tell her.

"I'm not naïve. I know my dad's been to prison," Phoebe said from the doorway.

Camille gestured for her to sit next to her on the bed.

"Just tell me," Phoebe said.

Camille sat there, looking at her strong, beautiful step-daughter.

"How much do you think you already know?" she asked Phoebe.

"Enough to know you're not like other parents. Which is cool. Enough to know that you and Dad aren't saints."

"Nobody is," Camille replied. "My father," she started to tell her then stopped.

"What about him? You've hardly told me anything about him, and when I asked, all you say is he died when you were too young. You never told me how he died though."

"He was murdered," Camille said quietly.

Phoebe sat up and looked at her in shock with her mouth open. "Oh my God, that's terrible. I'm so sorry."

"It was a very long time ago," Camille said. "I don't really think about it that much anymore. But when I was younger, I did."

"Is it okay if I ask how it happened?"

Camille nodded, but she wondered whether Johnny would be upset with her revealing the truth about them and about her father, and she considered that she was making a mistake. She told the girl anyway.

"My father was a gangster, and he was murdered because of that."

"What, like the mafia?"

"The Irish one, yes."

"That's crazy. Wait until all my guy friends find out. They're going to think it's really cool."

"Phoebe," Camille stopped her, "you can't go around telling anyone about us. The people in this town, in this neighborhood, they think we're just like them. You don't know how people will react if you tell them the truth. They could treat you, us, differently, badly. People can be very judgmental."

"Everyone in the neighborhood already saw you getting arrested," Phoebe said, rolling her eyes.

Camille sighed, knowing that was the truth. "Yeah, but your school friends don't need to know."

"Soon everyone will know," Phoebe said. "That's how it works in the suburbs, right? So, what's the point of hiding it?"

"If they're gonna find out on their own, we don't need to remind them."

"So why did the police arrest you? Dad tried telling me it was a misunderstanding, but I don't buy that."

Camille was silent, thinking about how to answer her. "There are things about us you don't know," she said, reasoning the girl was old enough for them to be honest with her.

"If this is about your sex life, I don't want to hear it," Phoebe said with a giggle.

"Phoebe," Camille scolded her. "Watch your mouth."

They had had "the talk" a couple of years ago.

"Sorry," Phoebe said, and gave her a sheepish look.

"There are things about us, complicated things, that you should know," Camille told her after a moment.

"What are they?" Phoebe asked, seeming somewhat afraid.

"Remember when we told you we run our own business?"

"Yeah, you're both always so busy."

"I know," Camille said with a smile, hoping that could change someday. "Well, the truth is sort of like that, we're business owners."

"But?" Phoebe said.

"But not everyone agrees with what we do for a living."

"Like the police?"

"Yes, you could say that."

"What do you do, anyway? Is it illegal?" Phoebe didn't seem as surprised as Camille assumed she'd be. But Camille didn't want to tell her more, because she didn't want to alter her perception of them too much.

She simply replied, "Some people don't like it."

"It's okay. I already figured it out a while ago. I just wanted you and Dad to tell me to my face."

"What? Really? You did?"

Phoebe nodded.

"You didn't tell anyone, did you?" Camille asked.

Phoebe shook her head. She didn't say anything, and Camille said, "Phoebe, promise me you won't say anything. It's very important."

"All right," Phoebe sighed. "Tell me about your dad."

Camille set her hands in her lap. "There's not much more to tell. I didn't get a chance to know him."

"Did he spend time in jail, like you and Dad?"

Feeling that honesty would be the best answer, Camille nodded.

"How long was he in jail?" Phoebe asked softly.

"A long time. From when he was very young."

"What did he do?"

"He killed someone, a terrible person who was hurting his sister."

"The guy deserved to die?"

"If anyone did, he did," Camille said with candor.

"What did the guy do to his sister?"

"He hurt her in the worst possible way you can hurt a woman."

"Oh," Phoebe said quietly, and Camille knew she'd understood what she'd meant. "I wish you could've known him."

"I do too," Camille said, and gave her a hug.

"Why were you beaten?" Phoebe asked her.

"That's a long, complicated story."

"Tell me, please."

"Someday when you're older."

Downstairs, Johnny met her at the landing with a cola in his hand.

"Did you two talk?" he asked Camille.

She nodded.

"And she's okay?" he asked.

"Yeah," Camille said. "I told her the truth about us."

"You what?" Johnny almost dropped the soda bottle on the floor.

Sheila came into the room from the kitchen to see what the commotion was about.

"Are you two arguing already?" she asked, a glass of wine in her hand.

"Camille told Phoebe what we do for a living," Johnny said.

Sheila gave her a look of surprise. "Now, why the fuck would she do that?"

"I don't know, but she did."

"I also told her about my father, who he was," Camille said.

"But I didn't say anything about yours," she said to Johnny. "I didn't go into details."

"Christ, I hope not. The girl's probably damaged enough already."

"Doesn't matter anyway. Because she already knew."

"What?" Sheila asked, drinking her red wine.

"Phoebe had already guessed what we do."

"How?" Johnny asked. "We're always so careful."

"She's a smart girl; she figured it out."

"I can't believe it," Johnny said.

"It's for the best," Sheila declared as she sipped her wine, looking Camille over. "Your face," she said to Camille after a moment. "I hope you get your looks back. Johnny, don't you hope so?"

"Yeah, yeah," Johnny said, though he didn't seem to be paying much attention.

Sheila walked up to Camille and stroked her face. "You were so pretty. I hope I haven't wrecked you for life."

"Looks aren't everything," Camille replied.

"It's nice to believe that, isn't it?" Sheila said, with a touch of bitterness, and Camille shook her head.

"I'm going to take a shower," she said.

16

Dana had received an interesting phone call from a detective named Seale, who asked to meet her at a café near the police station, alone, to talk. Apparently, Detective Seale had investigated Violet McCarthy and her mother, Catherine, who was now in prison, years ago. He was retired now, but heard about her investigation through a friend who was still on the force, and said he had some things he wanted to tell her, and she wanted to hear them.

Violet. Tommy's mother. Dana still hadn't decided what to do about Tommy. She didn't like lying to her superiors, but she didn't want to hurt Tommy either. She developed genuine feelings for him over the time they worked together.

Tommy didn't know about her meeting with Seale, and Dana didn't plan to tell him. She left the station at the end of the workday, and went straight to the café at the corner. She spotted the detective as soon as she entered, a tall, older man, handsome, with a couple of distinguished creases in his face that added to his charm, and thick, salt-and-pepper hair. He was wearing a dark suit without a necktie.

He seemed to recognize her right away, too.

"Detective Fitzpatrick?" he asked, waving her over.

Dana walked to his table, and he rose to shake her hand.

"Thanks for taking the time to meet with me," he said.

"No problem at all," she replied. "I'm very interested in hearing what you have to say."

"Likewise," he said as she sat down. Then he sat and asked her if she wanted a coffee. She saw that he'd waited until she arrived to order.

"Sure, that'd be great," she said. And he signaled for the waiter.

The waiter, a thin young guy, stepped over, and they ordered two coffees, but nothing to eat.

"Who do they have working the case with you?" Seale asked Dana, when the waiter had left their table.

"Oh, some uniform cop who wants to be a detective," she said without revealing too much.

Detective Seale chuckled. "They've got you playing babysitter, huh?"

"Yeah, something like that," Dana said with a smile, not wanting to give anything away about Tommy.

"Feels like a lifetime ago when I was still involved with all of that," he said, changing the subject, and she relaxed.

"I know what you mean," she said. "My father was in law enforcement, and he retired a few years ago."

"You come from a police family; that's very interesting. My father was a bit of a gambler, and he didn't much care for policemen. In my case, the apple *did* fall far from the tree."

Dana laughed politely at his joke.

The waiter returned with their coffees and after he'd left, Detective Seale asked her, "How much do you know about the McCarthys, their history in the neighborhood?"

"Only what I've read in the files," Dana answered honestly,

for she had never pressed Tommy for more information despite his connection.

"There's a lot of history, dating back to Catherine McCarthy's father, Violet's grandfather, Sean, who used to be the boss of the neighborhood. He ran the local racket, but was also involved in small-arms dealing, an all-around bad character. But perhaps what he's most known for around here, is being the murderer of Colin O'Brien, an up-and-coming gangster. Alleged murderer, that is. No charges were ever brought against him. Of course, the actual murder occurred out of our jurisdiction, in Los Angeles. This was during the '60s. Rumor has it that Catherine was also involved in O'Brien's death. They're an all-around very nasty family. I'd be careful if I were you. The grandfather was known to bribe law enforcement, and if he didn't get his way, he was known to ruin their careers in various ways, or eliminate them. Catherine was capable of similar things before she got sent away. I'm not sure about her daughter, but I would assume, in this instance, the apple doesn't fall far from the tree."

"I'm new around here," Dana said. "Who controls the area now? Violet? I mean, she and her boyfriend are running the local drug operation."

"No, that's the strange thing, because I heard it was Colin O'Brien's daughter, and her husband, Johnny Garcia, who control it these days. The daughter's mother, Sheila, is involved as well, apparently. Of course, this is just what I've heard over the years. I've never had it confirmed."

"What's her name, O'Brien's daughter?"

"Camille, I think. I don't know much about her. She's fairly secretive and keeps a low profile."

"I'm surprised she would allow Violet and Sam Paul to run a drug ring in her neighborhood," Dana thought out loud.

"Unless she's part of it?"

"No, I don't think she is. Maybe she doesn't know. And what

happens if she finds out?" Dana said, and Seale nodded solemnly, as if he knew she meant it would cause a gang war.

Colin O'Brien. He had to be the same man her mother had known, her mother's beloved friend who'd died tragically. In a way, she felt some affection for the man, as her mother had always talked so fondly of him.

"The thing you should know, and why I wanted you to come here, so I could tell you, is that you shouldn't underestimate the women in the McCarthy family. They're just as pure evil as the men. If I had to bet on it, I'd say that Violet is probably in charge of the ring, not her boyfriend."

"Really?" Dana said, feeling a bit guilty that she hadn't considered that.

"Sure," Detective Seale said. "During my years of work, one thing I learned is that the Irish mob are not as traditional as the Italians. It wouldn't surprise me if the whole thing was Violet McCarthy's idea, and Sam is just along for the ride."

"Just how evil is Violet McCarthy?" Dana asked, although she felt she already knew the answer.

"Years ago, she and her mother, they murdered a friend of mine," Seale replied. "Left his wife widowed. They'll do anything to get money, anything to get power. Not even the threat of Camille O'Brien is going to stop them from trying."

"You really think she's in charge of the whole drug operation? In my experience, it's usually the men in charge with the women assisting."

Detective Seale replied, "The McCarthy women aren't like most women involved in gangs. I'd be careful if I were you. If Violet McCarthy discovers you've been sniffing around, she's likely to send someone after you."

Dana sat there, quietly considering her own safety. What if Tommy told his mother they were onto her? He wouldn't do that, right? But truthfully, she didn't know him very well. She'd never been paranoid before, but she'd always been careful. And with Tommy, she'd slipped up.

"You must know them very well," she told Detective Seale.

"Yeah, they've remained a hobby for me for many years after my retirement."

"Are they a close family?"

"Yeah, they're as close as they come. They'd do anything for one another, kill, you name it. Violet has a son, but he fell of my radar when he became an adult. She's been with Sam Paul on and off for years. He isn't the father of her son though. Some Italian thug was. I forget his name. I don't think the son's involved with her activities or else I would've heard about it."

"Is Violet's son close to her?"

"I would assume so. They are a very close, secretive group."

Dana didn't say anymore, for fear of giving too much away. But, inside, she wondered, would Tommy be able to keep their work separate from his family? And what about a gang war? Dana didn't want one occurring on her watch, and so she couldn't risk Tommy giving his mother a head start.

She sighed and made casual conversation with Detective Seale as they finished their coffees.

And she left the café knowing what she had to do.

17

Did Tommy love Dana? He hadn't known her for long, but he felt that he might. No woman had ever made him feel that way before. Instant love. He'd never believed in that, he'd thought it was rubbish, until he met Dana. But why had he told her his secret so soon? Because he felt like he could trust her, although he hardly knew her? Even he didn't understand it. He hardly knew her, but he loved her.

He went into work in the morning, and he couldn't wait to see her. He'd brought them both a cup of coffee, but he didn't see her when he arrived. Something wasn't right in the station. Everyone became quiet and started looking at him when he entered. The whole place felt like someone had just died, and that someone was him. They'd looked as if they'd seen a ghost. What the fuck?

Tommy set the paper cups of coffee down on his desk, then Lieutenant Andrews stepped out of his office and said he wanted to speak with him.

"Yes, sir," Tommy said and left his coffee on the desk.

Where was Dana?"

"Should we wait for Dana? I mean, Detective Fitzpatrick?" he asked Andrews.

"No, I only need to see you," the lieutenant responded.

Tommy nodded and followed him into his office. What the hell was going on? Perhaps it was something good, like he was receiving his promotion early.

"Sit down," Andrews said without making the usual small talk.

"Sir, what's going on?" Tommy asked, his voice suddenly thickening with concern.

Tommy sat in the chair across from the lieutenant's desk. The lieutenant didn't sit down.

"I've known you for a long time, Tommy," he said, as he stared out his office window overlooking the city's skyline. "But I've never known that much about you."

"Sir, is everything okay?" Tommy asked, unable to disguise his apprehension. "I really don't understand what you're talking about."

"Your family, Tommy, I don't know anything about them, other than you're a local guy."

"There isn't much to tell," Tommy replied, hoping to drop the subject quickly. "They're just ordinary people."

"Just ordinary?"

"Yeah."

Lieutenant Andrews didn't speak when he finally sat down at his desk, across from Tommy, looking at him in silence. Staring the man face to face and lying to him was a lot harder than Tommy realized.

"You know, Tommy, to say I'm surprised by you would be an understatement," he finally spoke.

"I'm afraid I don't understand, sir."

Tommy glanced out the window that faced the rest of the station. Everyone seemed to have stopped working to watch him. They all seemed to already know something about him. But what?

"Tommy, Detective Fitzpatrick came to me earlier this morning with a very serious accusation," Andrews said bluntly.

"It was consensual," Tommy quickly replied, then saw from the look on Andrews' face that wasn't what he'd meant.

"Tommy, I don't care what you do outside my office as long as it doesn't interfere with work. But that isn't what I'm talking about."

"What do you mean?"

"Tommy, is it true that Violet McCarthy is your mother, and you have a different last name than her?"

It felt like all the air had been sucked dry from Tommy. It had never occurred to him that Dana would betray him. And why not? Because he'd loved her. Like a fool, he'd trusted her. Because he loved her. In the process, he'd broken the long-standing rule his mother had taught him: Never trust anyone outside of the family.

For a second, Tommy considered answering no. But what would have been the point? Now that Andrews knew the truth, he'd only find out more, and that would only make things worse for Tommy if he continued to lie.

Still, he couldn't believe Dana had betrayed him. "She told you?" he said to Andrews, his voice faint. Why had she?

"Of course she did; she's a good officer."

"What exactly did she say to you?"

"That you admitted to being Violet McCarthy's son," he said as if it were a curse.

"Did she tell you we got drunk and slept together, and I told her after?"

Andrews' face reddened and he shook his head. "She didn't mention that, no."

"And how is that okay, huh, her sleeping with her underling?" Tommy asked, suddenly furious with Dana.

"That's another matter."

"Yeah, well I hope you treat her accordingly," Tommy said bitterly, though he didn't really mean it. As angry as he was with Dana, he still cared about her, and he didn't want anything bad to happen to her. "Anyway, it's not what you think," Tommy said after a moment. "I haven't been helping my mother out during the investigation. I haven't done anything criminal. I haven't told her anything. I've been investigating her with Dana, with Detective Fitzpatrick, just like I would anyone else."

"But you didn't disclose to us that she's your mother. You continued to work on the investigation and chose not to excuse yourself. Why would you do that, if not to help her?"

"I didn't want anybody finding out that she's my mother," Tommy answered honestly.

"Tommy, I am so disappointed in you," Andrews said, setting his hands on the desk. "This was such a stupid thing for you to do. You had such a promising career ahead of you—"

"Had?" Tommy said.

"Now that I know the truth, I have to suspend you."

"Are you firing me?"

"I'm not sure what will happen, Tommy. This is very serious," he said somberly. "I need your gun and your badge."

"What will happen after?" Tommy asked, suddenly very worried, now that the whole thing seemed real.

"They'll be a hearing. A representative from your union will be there with you."

"I can't come to work in the meantime?" Tommy asked, because reality still hadn't really sunk in yet.

"Tommy, you're suspended. You can't come near this station. And stay away from Detective Fitzpatrick."

"That won't be a problem," Tommy said, although he knew it would be. He removed his badge and gun and set them on Andrews' desk. "Is that all, sir?" he asked.

"Yes, for now."

Tommy left the lieutenant's office and planned to get absolutely fucking drunk, but, first, he asked one of his colleagues if she had seen Detective Fitzpatrick.

"She just left," the woman replied.

"Shit," Tommy muttered under his breath and ran toward the exit.

He heard the woman say, "Is everything okay?" But he left without answering.

In the lobby, he saw Dana's gorgeous, shapely frame ascending down the large front steps. He tore open the door and ran after her.

"Dana, wait!" he shouted, not caring if he made a scene.

"Tommy, don't make a scene," she said to him over her shoulder, but she didn't stop walking. In fact, she walked faster.

"I don't care," Tommy said. "Dana, why? Why did you do it? I was in love with you."

"I cared about you, too, Tommy, but you should've known you shouldn't have asked me to keep a secret like that."

"Why did you do it, Dana? I cared about you. What about the night we spent together?"

"I'm sorry it happened," she said, and her words wounded him. "But I can't risk my entire career for you. What did you think we were going to do, run away together?" she said with an edgy, bitter laugh that jolted him.

"I would have run away with you," Tommy told her. "If you had asked me to, I would have." He neared her and reached out for her shoulder, grabbing her. "Dana, look at me."

Dana finally stopped walking and looked at him. "Well, I

wouldn't have done the same for you, Tommy. I'm sorry, but that's how it is." She shrugged her way out of his grasp. "Get off me," she said. "I actually have work to do."

The implication being that he didn't.

"You bitch!" Tommy shouted to her back as she left him, not caring who heard. "You cold, fucking bitch," he said faintly to himself, as he watched her walk away.

Then reality began to set in. He could forget about becoming a detective now. If the hearing didn't go his way, he could lose his job entirely. He began to panic and looked for the nearest pub, anywhere to get his mind off the situation fast.

Tommy settled on a rundown place on the next street, a place frequented by hardcore alcoholics as well as prostitutes and their pimps looking to get out of the cold for a few hours. The place had worn seats and shabby decorations on the walls.

Tommy stood out in the place like the cop that he was. Was. Tommy had to laugh about that. His career really might be in the past tense. He sat at the bar, alone, drinking shots of whiskey, avoiding the women who tried approaching him. His misery was such that he didn't even want to fuck anyone to help soothe him. Although that might change as the night wore on.

He liked this pub because the bartender never asked him if he'd had enough. The guy just kept pouring him drinks.

"Another?" the bartender said, and he poured him another drink anyway, before Tommy could answer. "Tough day?" he asked.

Tommy nodded.

"Feel like talking about it?" he asked, leaning against the counter.

Tommy glanced around the pub and saw that he was one of only a few patrons. It must have been a slow night. "No," he answered bluntly and kept drinking.

Tommy didn't want to make small talk tonight. He was at the pub for one reason: to get completely, absolutely, totally fucking smashed.

18

The bartender left the area, but returned every so often, to pour Tommy more drinks. After about an hour, a woman sat next to Tommy at the bar.

"Got a light?" she asked him, not long after she'd sat down.

Tommy didn't want to talk to anyone and didn't know if she was trying to pick him up, or what, so he ignored her.

"Hey, you got a light?" she asked him again, and he sensed she wouldn't shut up until he answered her, so he was forced to look at her.

Next to him sat a very attractive blonde woman, in a low-cut top. He couldn't believe how much she looked like Dana, and he did a double take.

"I don't smoke," he said when she continued looking at him, waiting for his answer, but he didn't smile, despite her beauty. Although, she certainly piqued his curiosity. What was a woman like her doing in this awful place alone? It occurred to him that she might be a prostitute, so he looked around for a pimp lurking nearby, but didn't see one.

"That's too bad," she replied, in a soft, beautiful voice. "I'm Pillow. What's your name?"

Her name made him smile. "Pillow? What kind of name is that?"

Pillow shrugged. "My mother gave all her children odd names. I have a younger brother named Cheese."

Tommy laughed, but she said, "I'm not kidding." He thought about giving her a false name, but then he told her, "I'm Tommy."

"Of course you are," Pillow said. "You look like a Tommy. What's a handsome guy like you doing in the bar in the daytime? Are you a cop?" she asked him. "Don't lie to me because I can tell."

"Yeah. How did you know?"

"You look like you don't belong in here, and the only people who come in here who look like they don't belong are usually cops trying to arrest us."

"For what?" Tommy asked. "I'm not here to arrest anyone; I'm just drinking tonight."

"They arrest us for existing," Pillow said, her voice suddenly very serious.

"Who is 'us'?"

"Us, prostitutes, pimps. What, did you think I was an angel?" Pillow laughed slightly, and he could see that a few of her teeth were discolored, though she was still beautiful.

"You look like an angel," Tommy said, flirting a little, because he was drunk. "Is your pimp around?"

"Why? You feel like buying me for the night?" Pillow leaned across and put her hand on his thigh.

Tommy stared at her hand on him.

"No, he isn't around. I came here to get away from this guy I live with."

"Why? Does he hurt you?" Tommy said, suddenly protective of her, though he didn't see any marks on her face.

Pillow shook her head. "He's a heroin addict, and sometimes

I just can't handle it. Need to be alone, so I come here to clear my head."

"Your pimp lets you have a boyfriend?"

"He's afraid of him."

"Your boyfriend's a tough guy, or what?"

"He used to be."

"Really?"

"Yeah. But they kicked him out of the mafia. Now he mostly gets high and watches TV."

"That's too bad. I'm sorry."

Pillow shrugged. "It's not your fault."

"Why does he get high? Did he have a bad childhood?"

Pillow shook her head. "No, he was in love with some woman, but she didn't want him."

Tommy sighed. "I can relate to that. What's your guy's name?"

"Billy," Pillow said. Then she said, "You got woman troubles?"

"Oh, yeah."

There was a warmness about Pillow that surprised him, and he felt like he could tell her anything, though he hardly knew her. In that way, she reminded him of Dana. Dana had betrayed him. He should be careful with this one too.

"Tell me about them, Tommy," she said, her voice soft.

"No, you don't want to hear my problems."

"I'm still here, aren't I? I got nowhere else to go. I got plenty of time to listen."

He didn't plan to tell her everything, although he knew he'd probably never see her again, and she wouldn't cause trouble for him.

"I was betrayed," he said, and took another drink.

"By your woman?"

Tommy nodded, and Pillow ordered a glass of white wine.

"Elegant," Tommy commented, about her choice of drink.

"For a whore?" Pillow replied with a smile that told him she wasn't really insulted.

Tommy chuckled slightly. "You seem pretty smart. How's a girl like you end up on the streets?"

"I'm not that smart," Pillow said. "I'm just experienced."

He figured she meant that she knew how to converse with men, that she knew the right things to tell them.

"Do you want to tell me about your childhood, Tommy?" Pillow asked.

"Not really," he replied.

"Good. Because I don't feel like telling you about mine. Other than my boyfriend and I, we aren't so different. We're alike, you see. Only after I stopped using, I couldn't get off the streets. So many years had passed by that I didn't know what to do."

"You don't seem old," he said.

She gave him a wink. "I bet I'm older than you." She paused then said, "Tell me about this girl of yours. How did she wrong you? She sleep with one of your friends?"

Tommy shook his head. "I can't say much other than she might have got me fired from my job."

"How the hell did she do that? She a cop too?"

Tommy nodded. "Yeah, she's older than me."

"An older woman. Interesting," Pillow said, with a little smile on her face. "You must have done something very bad, Tommy. Even I know that it's not easy for a cop to get fired."

"I made a mistake," he admitted.

"Why?"

"Because I didn't want anyone finding out something about me, about my family," he replied, and in his state of drunkenness he began to think of Pillow as his sort of therapist, someone to help him talk things through. But no matter how drunk he became, he'd never reveal the entire truth. He realized that his mother had taught him well, that protecting the family came first.

"It must have been something big," Pillow said, "for them to consider firing you. So, this woman, this girl of yours, she told them your secret?"

"Exactly," Tommy said, putting his head in his hand as the truth sank in.

"Why did you trust her with your secret, if it was so big?"

"I thought I loved her."

"You'd known her a long time?"

He shook his head, and then was embarrassed.

"Tommy, you're a romantic," Pillow said with another smile. "Didn't your mother ever tell you not to trust a girl until you know her well?"

"She did," Tommy said.

"But you didn't listen. This girl must really be something. Is she beautiful or what?"

"She is," Tommy said with a sigh.

"Maybe you were in love with her looks," Pillow suggested, and Tommy saw she'd nearly finished her glass of wine. More time had passed then he'd initially thought.

"No, it was more than that. She and I, we had a connection. At least, I thought we did."

"You did. Maybe she did too, or maybe she didn't."

Tommy nodded at her logic, although the words stung.

"Your family know about your troubles?" Pillow asked him after a moment.

Tommy wondered whether she'd order another drink and continue to sit with him.

Tommy shook his head. "I haven't told them yet."

"You got a father? A mother?"

"A mother," Tommy said. "My father died when I was young."

"Sorry to hear that. Is this secret about her, about your mother?"

"Sort of," Tommy said. "What about your family?" he asked her, not just to be polite, but because he was genuinely curious.

"It's not important," Pillow said, and he didn't bring it up again. "You're lucky you have a family. You should tell them what's going on. They can help you, because they know you best. They can help you more than I can." Pillow started to rise from her seat.

"You've already helped me," Tommy told her. "You've helped me more than you know."

Pillow smiled at him, and he knew she wouldn't stay for another drink. "Tommy, go see your family, go see your mother. I should be getting back to my guy, make sure he's doing okay. Go see your mother. Talk to her. She'll know what you should do, better than me."

"I will," Tommy said, as he waved goodbye to Pillow, somewhat regretting he hadn't asked for her phone number, though he'd come to think of her as someone who'd merely pass through his life just the one time. But he didn't want to talk with his mother, he wanted to confront her.

He watched Pillow walk away.

Where would Violet be at this hour? At the pub with Sam. Tommy had never really cared for his mother's live-in boyfriend, but he was surprised she hadn't married him after all these years. Then again, his mother had never married his father, either. Growing up, Tommy had viewed his father as a mysterious figure, as a man who'd wanted little to do with him over the years, and they had a scant relationship up until his father's death. But Tommy very much loved his mother, and they were very close. Which was why his disappointment about her return to her old ways had double the impact. Did she know what a burden it was to carry the McCarthy name? She knew he was a police officer, and what that meant, and how the connection between them could tarnish his career. It was bad enough to have the McCarthy name, and then she had to go and return to her old tricks? He was angry with Dana, but he was also angry with his mother. He'd known all his life that she wasn't a saint. But he'd thought all of that was behind her now.

Tommy made a fist and tapped it against the bar, thinking. He normally didn't mind a confrontation or a fight, but if there was one thing he dreaded, it was a confrontation with his mother. Not only did he hold her in the highest regard, he also feared her.

He paid his tab then drunkenly left the pub, looking around for Pillow outside, but she was long gone by then. He'd probably never see her again, and he somewhat regretted that, as despite having not known her for very long, he'd become fond of her.

He tried getting a taxi to stop, but it seemed nobody wanted to pick up a drunken man, so he slowly made his way to his mother's pub, wobbling as he did so. One of a group of tall young men elbowed Tommy as they made their way past him, laughing together.

"Fuck off," Tommy shouted at him, then remembered he wasn't a cop at the moment, nor did he have a gun.

"Shut up, old man," one of them said then had a laugh.

Old man? Old man! They were barely younger than him. But Tommy knew he wouldn't be any match for them in a fight. There were more of them, and he was drunk. Tommy continued on, hoping they would forget about him, but they turned around and followed him down the street as he walked.

"Fuck," Tommy mumbled to himself. He didn't need this shit, but it was following him anyway.

"Hey, you," one of the kids shouted at his back, and Tommy could feel them getting closer to him.

He turned around and said to the group, "I'm a cop. Back the fuck off."

The boys laughed.

"You ain't no cop," one of them said. "You're a fucking drunk."

"I am," Tommy replied over his shoulder, as he continued to walk down the quiet street. "Get the hell out of here. Go home."

"Maybe he is a cop," one of the boys whispered to the others. "Let's get the fuck out of here."

He relaxed a little when he turned around and saw them walking away in the opposite direction.

19

Tommy finally reached Violet's pub and found her setting up for the evening crowd inside. He hadn't greeted her upon entering, and just said, "Where's is he? Where's Sam?"

"Tommy," his mother said, putting down the glass she polished with a small white towel. She stepped out from behind the bar and seemed to want to give him a hug, but Tommy moved away from her so that she couldn't.

"Where's Sam?" he said, again. "What I have to say to you involves him as well."

"Tommy, are you drunk?" she said, staring at his face. "What are you doing, drinking so early? Shouldn't you be at work?"

"Yeah, I should be at work, but, thanks to you, I can't be."

"Tommy, I don't understand," Violet said, reaching out to touch his arm.

Tommy pulled away from her, as Sam stepped out of the backroom.

"Hi, Tommy," he said, keeping in line with the noncommittal politeness that had developed between them over the years.

"Tommy's drunk," Violet told Sam when Tommy didn't return his greeting.

"Oh. Is everything okay?" Sam asked.

"No, it isn't," Tommy said, moving closer to where they stood.

Violet looked around at the few customers they had in the place. "Tommy, can't this wait until afterhours?"

"No," Tommy said.

"Well, then, I'm going to have to ask you to not speak so loudly. It's hard enough to get business these days with so many new places moving into the area every day."

"Is that so? I would've thought business was great, why, with the high demand for your product in the area."

"Tommy, what are you talking about?" his mother asked him.

"You're really going to stand there and lie to me?" Tommy said.

Sam looked at Violet and said, "I think we should go into the kitchen to talk about this."

"See, he knows what I'm saying," Tommy told his mother.

They moved into the kitchen where the cook hadn't arrived yet for the night, and Tommy leaned against one of the counters with his arms crossed, while Sam and Violet stood opposite him.

"Tommy, you're scaring me. What the hell is going on?" Violet asked him. "Why aren't you at work? Are you ill or just drunk?"

"I'm not at work because of you and because of him," Tommy replied, glancing at Sam.

"What are you talking about, Tommy?" Violet said, and made him feel like a small boy again. "Sam and I haven't done anything wrong."

Tommy laughed like a mad man. "I might lose my job because of you!" he shouted. "After grandma got sent to prison, you promised me you were done with your old ways, but you're not. You never were."

"Tommy, that's the truth. The past is behind me; I promise

you," Violet said, but Sam seemed to comprehend they'd been caught.

Sam touched Violet's arm. "I think he's saying he knows, V, about what we're doing."

Violet stood there in silence, staring at Tommy like she'd seen a ghost. "What does that have to do with your job being at risk?" she finally said.

Tommy didn't know how much he should tell her, how much he could tell her.

"Tommy, how do you know? What's going on? Tell me," Violet said, approaching him and grabbing his arm.

Tommy pulled away and shook his head then he left the kitchen, ignoring his mother as she ran after him, calling his name. He avoided her grasp and looked over his shoulder to see Sam restraining her as she raged at him.

Tommy knew what his legacy was, and, so far, he'd managed to avoid it, but now everything was catching up to him, and he didn't know for how much longer he could live an ordinary life.

~

Camille wore her only suit to the prosecutor's office. It was the one she usually wore to Mass on Sundays or to funerals. And with her sleek black cane at her side, she felt like she was back to being her old self.

She'd been called to the office by Mickey, and she'd only seen the prosecutor one time previously, in court, and the woman hadn't seemed to like her very much. In fact, the woman seemed like a mean bitch and looked the part.

Johnny donned one of his many fine suits to accompany her there, but they took one of their more modest cars, so as to not draw too much attention to themselves. Mickey was forever advising her to always seem humble in the eyes of the law, and that certainly didn't include zipping about in a Ferrari, though Johnny owned two.

Once they arrived, they had to park in an underground garage and then get past security. Mickey hadn't told Camille what was going on exactly, but she knew it had something to do with her case. Camille suspected that even Mickey didn't know, or perhaps he did and didn't want her to get her hopes up too much. She wondered if they'd offer her a plea deal, but she really didn't want to spend any more time away from her family behind bars and away from her business.

Mickey met them in the lobby, once the security officers checked them for weapons.

"What's going on, Mickey?" Johnny asked him, as eager for news as Camille was.

"Even I don't know," Mickey replied. "They called me in here this morning and asked you to come along."

Then something occurred to Camille, something she really didn't like. "I hope they aren't gonna ask me to snitch on anyone." Camille didn't know how much the prosecutor's office knew about her and Johnny's lifestyle and their business, as they kept a low profile, but they must've known something about it.

"I'm not sure, Camille," Mickey said, swinging his briefcase lightly in his hand. "But you might consider it, if they do."

Camille glanced at Johnny, and wondered what his thoughts were. She knew he wouldn't want her to be sent away from him and Phoebe again.

They rode the elevator upstairs with Mickey and then sat in the prosecutor's waiting room until she called them inside. Camille looked around the room while she waited, squeezing Johnny's hand. She wondered what it would be like to be the prosecutor. After all, the woman had a lot of power, and, probably, a lot of money. But Camille knew she'd never be able to send her friends away to jail, although it would be nice to send a few enemies there, she thought with a smile.

Johnny noticed her look. "What's on your mind?" he asked her, seeming to find her smile strange, given the situation.

"I was just thinking how I wouldn't mind seeing Violet McCarthy sent packing," Camille whispered to him, glancing at the prosecutor's secretary, who was staring at her from her desk in the corner. Camille wanted to ask her what the hell she was looking at, but she didn't think that would go over well with the prosecutor.

After what felt like hours, but was only about 30 minutes, the prosecutor's office door opened, and the tall, thin, elegant white-haired woman emerged. Mickey quickly rose and shook her hand. The woman looked at Camille and Johnny, both now stood and nodded. Camille nodded back, and even gave her a smile. She figured it couldn't hurt to play nice. The prosecutor didn't return the gesture, and Camille was left feeling slighted. But what had she expected? The law would never be her friend.

The prosecutor escorted them inside her office, with an expansive view of the river that was illuminated by the sunshine. Camille sat down next to Mickey and Johnny and looked at the glittering water. The prosecutor cleared her throat and Camille turned her attention back to the matter at hand.

The woman sat behind her polished desk as if sitting at a throne. Camille smirked to herself at the image.

"Does something amuse you, Mrs. Garcia?" the prosecutor asked her.

Shit, Camille thought. She didn't like this woman, but she could make Camille's life a living hell.

"No, sorry," she murmured.

The prosecutor stared at her for a moment then looked at Mickey. "Thank you for bringing your client here today."

"Of course," Mickey said, giving her the smile he used when

he wanted something, a look Camille knew well. "Thank you for seeing us."

"I'll cut right to the chase," the prosecutor said to them. "Today's your lucky day," she told Camille.

Camille sat there, still not believing what she was hearing, and to think, she'd entered thinking it would be something awful.

"Excuse me?" Camille said, stunned.

"You've been deemed a non-violent offender," the prosecutor told her.

Camille wanted to smile at the irony, at how much the woman didn't know, but she restrained herself. "I don't understand," she said, looking at Mickey but not wanting to seem too surprised.

"My office has a backlog of cases so we've decided not to bother with yours, with a trial and such, if you accept a plea deal with time served."

"I won't have to return to prison?"

"That's correct," the woman said with a sigh.

"Baby, did you hear what she said?" Johnny told Camille as she sat there quietly. He rose and wanted to embrace her, but she found herself unable to move.

When she finally did move, the prosecutor had taken a phone call, and waved them out of her office. Johnny went to embrace her again in the lobby and this time she accepted. Mickey also gave her a hug.

"I have to say, you're fucking lucky, Camille," he said with a grin.

But Camille didn't believe in luck, at least not in the traditional sense, and she especially didn't believe in saying aloud how lucky you were, for fear it could jinx you.

"Don't say that," she told Mickey. "You know how I feel about that."

"Yeah, sorry, but you are."

"Let's go out to celebrate," Johnny said. "Mickey, you're coming with us."

Mickey agreed to go, and they planned to meet at a restaurant down the street. After a long meal and plenty of drinks, Johnny and Camille said goodnight to Mickey who lived alone, and then drove home to the suburbs.

As Camille and Johnny approached their house, she saw that strange car parked nearby and pointed it out to him.

"What the fuck?" Johnny said. "What does this guy think he's doing?" He slowed the car down and parked farther away from their home.

"Wait here," he told Camille as he opened the driver's side door with the engine still running.

"Johnny—" Camille said, wanting to go with him.

"Stay here," he said, as if he thought the driver could be dangerous. Normally, someone might call the police in the same situation, but Camille and Johnny preferred handling such things themselves.

Camille nodded as he closed the door and watched him from inside the car. Johnny slowly walked toward the strange vehicle, but as he went closer to it, the driver took off, speeding away down the street, tires screeching. Johnny grabbed the closest object he could find, a somewhat large rock, and hurled it at the back of the car, barely missing it.

"Fucker!" he screamed at the car as it disappeared into the evening.

Camille got out of their car and ran up to him.

"Do you think it's cops spying on us?" she asked him, touching his shoulder.

Johnny turned and looked at her. "I'm not sure, but whoever it is, they got some nerve. We're gonna find out who it is. Nobody fucks with us. If it's that Billy, he's gonna be a dead man soon."

"Don't say that," Camille replied, suddenly defensive of Billy, her first love. "It's not him; he wouldn't do something like that."

"He was fucking obsessed with you, baby. He still is, for all we know. It's him."

"No," Camille said, shaking her head. "The last I heard, he was too messed up to even leave the house."

"It's him. I just know it. He's fucking dead," Johnny said loudly.

Camille shushed him, suddenly aware of their quiet suburban neighborhood. By now, their neighbors already thought they were trouble. She didn't need them thinking anything worse. She also still cared about Billy, and knew what Johnny could do.

"Let's go inside," Camille said to Johnny. "Phoebe and my mother will want to know we're home." Sheila had stayed with the girl while she and Johnny went out with Mickey.

Johnny nodded. "I'll go inside," he said, returning to their car with her. "But if it is Billy, he's finished."

His words shook Camille, but she couldn't let him know how much they frightened her. As far as Johnny knew, Billy was in her past, but sometimes Camille wasn't sure.

Tommy's absence left a void in Dana's day. She had gotten used to him over the past weeks, had gotten used to having a partner. Now she was solo. And Tommy? What would happen to him?

Dana knew he could lose his job, that it was a very real possibility. She tried not to think about Tommy's fate, because doing so upset her. After all, she wasn't made of ice. The hardest part was that she had to focus on work; she had to solve the drugs case. She knew she could do it on her own, she knew that she was capable, but she couldn't stop thinking about how she'd betrayed Tommy. They'd both used each other, but she cared about him. Her decision to go to his boss hadn't been easy, but police work was in her blood, and if there was one thing her father taught her, it was that the law came first. She suspected that might not be true of Tommy, and his revelation to her about his mother had concerned her. At the end of the day, Dana felt she had made the right decision, and that was how she continued to function.

Now came the hardest part, to continue on with work as if Tommy had never been there. But Dana went about her duties, and one afternoon she parked some distance from Violet McCarthy's pub, where she still had a view of the alleyway behind it, and she waited. She had a plan that she wanted to test out.

Dana waited for hours. She had the radio on at low volume, but she wasn't listening to it, it merely filled the void that Tommy had left. She waited until dawn nearly arrived, and she saw Sam Paul exiting the back entrance of the pub with the trash he carried out to the alley every late night after closing. Dana had been staking out the place over the past few nights, and she'd come to notice a pattern, that Sam always left after Violet, that he stayed on to carry out the closing duties.

Dana quickly shut off the radio and stepped out of her car, closing the door lightly. She approached Sam slowly, so as not to alarm him. He had his back to her as he moved the full garbage cans around, but then turned around fast when she stood behind him.

He took a step back, recognizing her immediately. "What are you doing here?"

"I'm here to talk with you, Sam," Dana replied, and showed him her badge, although he already knew who she was.

"What do you want?" Sam asked.

Dana had wondered how much Tommy had told Sam and his mother about their investigation, if he'd told them anything, but now she knew he hadn't, and that wounded her. It seemed Tommy had done the right thing after all. Perhaps she'd judged him too harshly, and she had a touch of regret about going to his boss.

"Sam, do you have a moment?" she said.

"I'm closing for the day," he replied, returning to his task. "I'm sorry, but I can't help you."

Dana had wanted to get him on his own without Violet. She knew about the time he'd spent in prison, and about his assault there, and that he'd do anything to avoid serving more time. Of the two, she reasoned Sam would be the easiest to break, and with what Detective Seale had said about Violet being the leader.

"Sam, it's in your best interest for you to speak with me," she told him.

"You have some nerve," he said, turning to her again, displaying an angry side that she didn't know he had. "You have some nerve sneaking up on me like this, even if you are the police."

"Sam, I have a proposal for you," she said, looking around to confirm they were alone. "I want you to consider helping me."

"You mean you want me to snitch on her, on Violet?"

Dana nodded. "I know about your record, Sam. You don't want to return to prison, which is where you're going to end up sooner or later because we're going to catch you two. So I'm asking you to consider helping us out, and in exchange, I'll speak with the District Attorney on your behalf, and you can avoid prison."

"What makes you think I'll turn against her? She and I, we've been together for a long time. I love her; I love her to death."

"Sam, remember what prison was like for you? You still have your golden boy good looks; it's going to be even worse for you in there this time around," Dana said, hoping to push him over to her side.

Sam scowled at her. "You're a sick person," he told her. "You cops, you think you can do whatever you want to get your way. If there's one thing I've learned over the years, that's it."

"Those guys who assaulted you, I heard they're still serving time. You do know you'll be sent to the same prison once you're convicted?" she said to him, although she wasn't certain. "I bet they're just waiting to have another go at you."

Then his face changed, going from pale to reddening. He was quiet while he seemed to be thinking. Thinking really hard. "This deal you're offering," he said after few moments. "Is there an expiration date on it?"

Dana shook her head. "But I'll need to know your answer sooner rather than later."

"How do I get in touch?"

She handed her card to him. "You can give me a call."

Sam wiped his brow and accepted the card.

21

Through Anton, Camille and Johnny had arranged a meeting with Violet McCarthy's supplier. Although Violet was encroaching on their territory, and they were certainly within their rights to act, they'd decided on a meeting for now, rather than an all-out gang war, to stake their claim on the neighborhood.

The supplier, a man called the Swede, worked out of a renovated warehouse on the riverfront. Camille and Johnny parked outside the address Anton had given them, and waited for him to arrive. They had arranged to meet the Swede in the evening, and the sunlight faded above the water, casting a subtle glow over its shores.

"What a beautiful night," Johnny commented to her as they waited. "Camille?" he said, when she didn't answer him.

"Sorry," Camille finally replied. "But you know how I get before big meetings."

"I know. I'm the same way," Johnny said, putting his arm around her and pulling her in close. "At least we came prepared," he said, patting his gun at his side.

Camille spotted Anton's blue Mercedes in the rearview

mirror and watched him pull up into the secluded, gravel-strewn area where they were parked.

"Here he comes," she told Johnny.

Anton parked, stepped out of his car, and approached Johnny's window. He tapped on the glass, and Johnny rolled the window down.

"You ready?" Anton asked them.

Johnny nodded, and he and Camille exited their car, meeting Anton outside. They approached the building as a group, and then Anton stopped in front of a large red door of the nondescript warehouse and made a call on his cell phone.

"We're here," he spoke into his phone.

After a moment, the door opened, and a hulking bald man dressed in black came outside to greet them.

"Please follow me," he said politely to the three of them.

Once they were inside the place, Camille noticed it seemed very professional, like an actual office, not an old warehouse. A second man approached them, also hulking.

"I need to check you for weapons," he said in a flat tone, and seemed the type of person who rarely smiled.

Johnny looked to Anton. Camille knew he didn't like entering unknown territory without backup in the form of a weapon, but since they were on the Swede's turf, they would have to play by his rules. Anton had told them that the Swede was a very powerful person who had connections to the cartels and the mafia, so she and Johnny wanted to show him respect, as well as let him know they—not Violet—owned the neighborhood. Owning one neighborhood in the city wasn't much from an outside perspective, but it had been quite profitable for them over the years, and she and Johnny wanted to keep it that way.

"You can search me," Johnny told the man. "But I can already tell you I got a gun. My wife, she's got one on her too."

"I'm gonna need to take them," the guy replied to Johnny. Then he looked at Anton. "You got one on you? If so, I'm gonna need it."

Anton nodded and handed his gun over to the man.

Camille stood there, shivering in the very cold building. They must've had the air conditioning down fucking low.

Anton waited patiently as the guy patted him down, then Johnny handed his gun over, and the guy patted him.

He stopped when he came to Camille. She reluctantly handed hers over to him, but Johnny shouted, "Don't you fucking touch her," when the man began to pat her down, a little too slowly for his liking.

"Hey, hey," another man shouted as he approached them. "Are we going to have a problem here or what?" he said.

Camille turned to look at the man who'd spoken, a tall, youngish, fit man, with striking, fair good looks. Before he even introduced himself, she knew he must be the Swede.

"I don't want him touching my wife. He seems like he's enjoying it a little too much," Johnny said to the Swede.

"All right, all right." The Swede spoke to Camille, "Did you hand in your gun?"

Camille nodded.

"Have anything else on you?" he asked her, his breath smelling strongly of tobacco.

"No," she said, and she saw that he'd taken her word for it because she was a woman. Which could have been a big mistake.

"Then we're all good here," he spoke to his men, his words an order. "Welcome to my home," he told Johnny and Camille. Then he exchanged pleasantries with Anton, whom he seemed to know well. His clearly armed men followed closely behind them as he led the group into the inner part of the building where there were white leather couches and a very large television in a room with a pool table. There were pieces of artwork on the walls, which Camille assumed must have been expensive.

The Swede motioned for his men to leave then asked the group to sit down. Obviously, he felt confident enough to be alone with them.

"Any of you care for a drink?" he asked, walking to the small bar in the room.

Johnny and Camille sat down and glanced at each other. She sensed both wanted to remain alert and sober for the meeting, so they declined. Anton sat next to them and said yes to a drink.

"Vodka with cranberry?" the Swede asked Anton, which Camille knew was his favorite drink.

Anton accepted the drink with thanks, and the Swede took a seat on the couch opposite them. Camille could feel Johnny shifting next to her, and reasoned he must have been as eager as she was to begin the conversation.

"I think it's no secret that we're here today because I know Anton," the Swede said, sipping his drink.

"We've got no problem with you," Johnny told him. "It's Violet McCarthy we have troubles with."

"Violet," the Swede said with a chuckle.

"She isn't supposed to be dealing in our neighborhood, and she knows it," Camille spoke up.

The Swede stared at her with an amused expression on his face. "I was surprised to see you brought your woman with you," he said to Johnny. Camille noticed he had a very slight accent, as though he came to the country as a child.

"Camille's a part of this, too," Johnny replied.

"Camille. Violet. We've got lots of powerful women in this city," the Swede said, with a smile like before, that made Camille want to slap him. He paused and seemed to only look at Johnny when he spoke. "You want me to stop supplying Violet and start supplying you?"

Johnny nodded.

"That'd be very disrespectful to Violet," the Swede said.

"We can handle her," Camille replied. "We have before."

"I don't doubt it," he said, grinning at her. If Johnny hadn't been in the room, Camille imagined he would have winked at her. "You're not going to give me a choice, are you?"

Johnny seemed hesitant to agree, and Camille felt the same way, as agreeing would mean that they were willing to start a war with the Swede and his associates. But the possibility hung there in the air, for some time, as Anton sipped his drink next to them and the Swede sat there, looking at them.

"If I might be frank," Johnny suddenly said. "It was bold of you to sell to Violet. You must know that Camille and I control the neighborhood."

The Swede gave him a slight smirk and touched his gun at his side. "Are we going to have a problem? Do I need to call my men back in here?" He chuckled a little.

"No problem," Johnny said. "All I'm saying is that you must have known this could happen, when you did what you did. We can give you some time, but not very much."

"You must realize this puts me in a difficult situation."

Johnny gave him a shrug like that wasn't their problem. "Like I said, we can give you some time, but not much."

"I don't think there's much of a decision to make," the Swede replied thoughtfully. "It's you or we go to war, correct?"

"I'm sure you already know the answer," Johnny said, then he looked at Camille and gestured that it was time for them to leave.

Camille followed him, and Anton rose to say goodbye to his friend. Outside, Johnny spoke to Anton about the situation.

"What do you think he'll do?"

"He's a smart guy. He'll work with you; I'm confident."

"If he doesn't, if he sticks with McCarthy, then how fucked are we gonna be?" Johnny asked Anton bluntly.

Camille knew he meant that it could allow Violet to take control of the neighborhood again.

"That's not gonna happen," Anton told them.

But Camille wasn't convinced.

22

One morning, the phone rang while Tommy was still asleep. He answered, and heard a woman's voice. For a moment, he thought it was Dana and his heart leapt. Then his mother said, "Tommy?" and his joy collapsed.

"What do you want?" he asked her, risking her wrath by being impolite to her.

"Tommy, don't you talk to me that way," she snapped back. "You may be mad at me, but I'm your mother. Show me some damn respect."

Tommy didn't say anything, and his mother continued talking. "What's going on with you? I sense there's more to the story than what you told Sam and me. Are you having woman troubles?"

As usual, she was right. But he didn't want her to know he'd become close to Dana, that he had fallen for her, and because of that, he had betrayed his mother. He didn't want her to know his failing.

"I know how much your job means to you, Tommy. I may not understand why you love being a cop so much, but I respect it. I'm sorry to hear what happened."

His mother loathed the police so much that Tommy knew how difficult it must have been for her to say that. "I appreciate that," he said.

She was his mother, his blood, and she loved him, and Tommy thought of all the things she had done for him over the years, how she had raised him alone when his father abandoned him, how she had overcome addiction to retain custody of him, her only son, how she would do anything for him. He might not have cared what happened to Sam, but he very much cared what happened to Violet. Keeping the truth from her would hurt her, because he felt that, Dana, being a competent policewoman, would catch Sam and Violet, sooner rather than later. He couldn't see his mother sent away, like his grandmother had been, despite knowing that to tell her the truth meant he could lose his job. Violet was set in her ways, and even her son couldn't change her. But he could help her.

"You're being investigated," he told Violet. "You and Sam, you both are, for dealing heroin in the neighborhood."

"By who? You?" Violet laughed slightly, but when Tommy didn't reciprocate, she said, "Tommy, tell me you didn't."

"I'm sorry, but I did. That's why I got suspended. They found out I'm related to you."

"I knew you didn't talk about me at work, but how did they find out?"

"It's not important," Tommy told her.

"I can't believe you betrayed me, your own mother."

Tommy had made a decision, and he knew there was no going back.

"I know I did," he said. "But I'm telling you now."

"You're putting your job on the line for me," she said. "I never thought you'd do that. But I did always tell you that the most important thing is family. Who's working with you? I assume you aren't on your own."

"They had this female detective, Fitzpatrick, with me."

"She any good?"

"Yes, very. That's why I knew I needed to warn you."

"How much does she know?"

"Enough," Tommy said.

"You did the right thing, telling me," Violet said.

But a surge of guilt overcame Tommy and he had an unsettling feeling in his stomach. He shifted in bed, and sat up, putting his head in his hands.

"Tommy?"

He sighed and said, "I'm still here."

"What you said has got me thinking," Violet told him in a whisper. "Something's been off about Sam lately."

"What do you mean? Is he there now?"

"No, he stepped out for a while. He hasn't been his usual self. He's been avoiding me."

"You think she, Fitzpatrick, got to him?" Tommy asked.

"I'm not sure. Maybe I'm just overreacting. But you know how my feelings are never wrong."

If Dana got Sam to turn against Tommy's mother, then Dana could put Violet away for life. And Sam would probably escape with a minor scolding.

"That fucker," Tommy seethed, rage filling his veins, and the pressure increasing in his head.

"He'd do anything to avoid prison again, after what they did to him on the inside. I know that much."

"I can't believe he'd betray you like that."

"I love him, and I don't like to think it. But I just have this feeling." She paused. "What are you going to do about it, Tommy? You have to protect me, Tommy. I'm your mother."

Tommy tried to disguise his sighing as dread filled his mind.

23

Violet ended her call with Tommy. What would Tommy do about Sam? Despite their differences about his career, Tommy was very much Violet's son.

"Violet," a man said as he entered. She looked up to find the Swede.

Violet hadn't been expecting him, and his presence alarmed her. He didn't seem like the kind of guy who just dropped by unexpectedly to say hello.

"What's going on?" she asked him, looking around the empty pub. They had just opened for the day, but it was so early that even the daytime drinkers hadn't arrived yet. Whatever the Swede had to tell her, it must have been quite important for him to arrive so early.

Despite the place being uncrowded, she escorted him into the dim backroom, but, without Sam, kept her guard. Besides, the Swede knew Violet was really in charge of the operation, not Sam. There was a gun behind some boxes within her reach.

"We have a problem," he told her.

"I figured as much, that's why you're here."

"I've worked with you, as a favor to my sister, because she

and your mother are both serving time together," he said, and Violet waited for the "but".

"This couple, Camille and Johnny Garcia, they own your neighborhood. You told me they wouldn't be an issue, that you were in with them. Turns out, you're a fucking liar," the Swede said, barely able to keep his cool. "They want nothing to do with you."

Violet took a step back. "I didn't think they'd find out," she said quietly. "Have they?"

"Oh, yeah. You were damn stupid, Violet. They fucking know everything, and, now, they want a piece of the action. They want me to ditch you for them."

"Or else?"

"Or else they're going to start a war with me, you crazy bitch!" He put his hand to his forehead and growled. "I don't need this shit."

"Are you—are you going to work with them?" she asked, knowing that if she lost him, she'd lose her business.

"You mean am I willing to risk it for you?" The Swede laughed manically.

"I can make it worth your while," she said, approaching him. She wasn't that young anymore, but she still had her looks. Sam would understand, she reasoned, and if he wasn't going to be around for much longer anyway, then she had to look out for herself.

"I don't want you," the Swede told her, pushing her away.

Violet nearly fell to the floor, and she straightened herself and gave him a look of disgust. "You bastard, you could've knocked me over," she hissed.

"Shut up," he said, stabbing his finger at her.

Violet regretted shutting the door to the room. Could she reach for the gun fast enough?

"Sam will be back soon," she told him to remind him she

wasn't on her own. "People will be arriving soon, to drink," she added. Then she almost said, "You can't do anything to me, not with someone else around," but she stopped herself, because she didn't know how much of a risk taker he was.

The Swede stood there, looking as though he wanted to hit her. Then he seemed to consider her words. "What are you going to do about our predicament? It's up to you to solve it. I ain't doing shit."

"Don't worry," Violet assured him, sweat wetting her brow uncomfortably. "I'll handle it."

Camille had been her greatest enemy, and now it looked as though she was again, and if there was one thing Violet knew very well, it was that she wasn't easy to get rid of.

24

After her good fortune, Camille promised herself that she would spend more time with her family. Phoebe, especially. The evening was warm and pleasant, so she decided to walk with the girl to the movie theatre in their small town, and see a film that she knew Johnny wouldn't like.

"Are we going to see a girl movie?" Phoebe asked her as they strode on the quiet street.

"Yeah. How'd you know?" Camille said with a smile.

"I could tell because Dad didn't ask to come with us," she said with a giggle.

"It's true; he hates romantic movies."

"But he seems very romantic with you!" Phoebe said with a laugh.

"Ah, you're too young to notice those things," Camille said.

"Hardly. I'm a teenager, remember?"

"Don't go thinking about boys too much. Enjoy this time of your life while you can, but don't go crazy. You'll be my age before you know it." Camille grinned.

"No!" Phoebe said in horror. "What were you like at my age? Grandma never told me."

"I wasn't a slut, if that's what you're asking, but I wasn't exactly a good Catholic girl."

Phoebe giggled at her step-mother's choice of words, and before Camille knew it, they had arrived at the theatre, to find a long queue already out front for the popular, new film.

Phoebe grumbled, but they stood behind the others and waited. Phoebe became quiet, surrounded by groups of kids her age, as though she was embarrassed to be seen out with her step-mother. It had taken a lot of effort on Camille's part to get Phoebe to go in the first place.

"Worried your friends will see us?" Camille asked her with a smile.

Phoebe shrugged, and Camille could tell she didn't want to talk about it.

Camille loved her stepdaughter with all her heart, and while she was waiting, she had plenty of time to contemplate the past few weeks. What would have happened to Phoebe if Camille had been sent away to prison for a long time? Johnny would have continued to raise her, with Sheila's help. But a girl needed a mother, and Sheila wouldn't be around forever. Phoebe had already lost her own mother so young. Camille dreaded thinking about what might have been.

Eventually, they got to the ticket box, and got the last two tickets for the film. She'd been lucky again. Camille felt that too much good luck would eventually bring bad luck, and, suddenly, she wanted to hold Phoebe very close.

"Come here," she said, putting her arm around the girl as they walked inside the theatre, stopping to buy popcorn.

"Ma, I'm too old for that," Phoebe said, stepping out of her reach.

"I know; I just want to hug you."

"Well, you just did."

Camille didn't want to push her luck, so she gave up trying

once more, and they managed to find two seats near the back of the crowded theatre. They talked a little about Phoebe's school, and then the lights faded, and the movie started.

Afterwards, Camille considered ringing up Johnny at home to ask him to give them a ride back to the house, as it was relatively late, but since the weather was still pleasant, she decided to walk home.

Few cars were out on the road, but as they were nearing their street, a car slowly approached, in an area without streetlamps. The car looked somewhat familiar to Camille, but in the darkness, she couldn't be sure.

"Think they need directions?" Phoebe asked her innocently.

"I don't know, sweetheart." She had gone to the theatre unarmed, as she disliked carrying her gun in public, unless she attended a meeting relating to her and Johnny's business dealings.

The car sped up then stopped quietly in the road up ahead. Something definitely wasn't right. Camille searched the area frantically for an escape, and saw nothing but row after row of dark houses, with occupants asleep for the night. It had been a treat for Phoebe to go out to see a movie on a weeknight.

"Phoebe," Camille ordered, fear thick in her voice. "Stay behind me."

"What's going on?" Phoebe said, frightened by her step-mother's words.

Someone exited the car, wearing dark clothing and a ski mask. In the dark, Camille couldn't tell their gender. An object glinted in their hand, something long. She looked closely and saw that it was a big knife.

Her heart pounded fast as she grabbed Phoebe's hand. There was no time to think, they had to move. "Phoebe, run!"

Even if Camille didn't escape, then maybe at least Phoebe could. But Phoebe panicked and ran out into the street, and right into the arms of the knife-wielding figure. Camille bolted toward them, screaming Phoebe's name.

It was Phoebe they were after, not her.

"You fucking let her go, you bastard! I'm gonna fucking kill you!" Camille yelled at the top of her lungs

The figure pushed Phoebe inside, then got into the driver's seat and sped away, as Camille pounded on the window, tires screaming. She chased after the car as it left, but quickly lost them. Although she did catch the last three letters of the license plate. Z51.

She'd lost her. She'd lost Phoebe.

Frantic, with tears streaming down her face, Camille raced home, banging on the door with her fists for Johnny to let her inside, unable to use keys in her state of despair.

She kept repeating in her mind, "Z51." It had to have something to do with Violet.

"Camille, what the fuck is going on?" Johnny said when he opened the door. "Where's Phoebe?"

"Someone took her, Johnny. They fucking stole her right in front of me, the bold bastards."

Johnny went very pale, looking like all the life had left him, and like he could collapse to the ground. "No!" he shouted. "Who did it? Who was it?"

Camille shook her head. They had plenty of enemies among them.

"It's Violet. It's her. It's because we went to her supplier," Johnny insisted.

"That's the first thing I thought, too," Camille said.

"We need to go after the bitch! Now!"

"Johnny, I saw some of the license plate. We gotta think with our heads first, and find out who owns the car to be sure."

"Was it the same car, the one that's always outside our house?" Johnny asked her.

"No, Billy would never do such a thing," Camille said, knowing what he was thinking. "I dunno if it was the same car, Johnny. It was dark. I couldn't tell. But I do know Billy would never harm Phoebe."

Camille started to sob, and Johnny embraced her, holding her tightly against his chest, whispering that everything would be okay.

They didn't go to the police directly. They didn't trust the police.

But they did have someone who worked for the police department on their payroll, and Johnny was on the phone with the guy no more than a few seconds later.

"What did he say?" Camille asked him after he'd ended the call, from where she sat on the living room sofa, occasionally drinking from a small glass of whiskey that Johnny had given her to calm her.

"He said he'd ring me back in an hour or so. He's got to look up the numbers first," Johnny replied about the license plate Camille had given him.

25

The hour-long wait was one of the most agonizing experiences Camille had ever suffered, not knowing where Phoebe was or even if she was still alive. Johnny looked ill too, but he was a strong man and didn't like showing it, so he sat with Camille, with his arm around her as he had the television on, staring at it quietly, not really watching the program.

By the time the phone rang, Camille didn't have any tears left. Both jumped up from the sofa at the ringing sound, and Johnny answered.

Camille listened in on the conversation. "Yeah?" A pause. "That's the last name on the registration? Are you fucking kidding me?" Johnny hung up and stared at Camille.

"Johnny, what the hell is going on?" she asked him.

Johnny looked confused and a little frantic. "Camille, you're not gonna fucking believe this, but the car is registered to Marie Russo."

"Russo?" Camille repeated quietly. She only knew one person with the surname. Her former step-father, Vito. The man who had tried to sexually assault her when she was a teenager, the man her mother had divorced, after Camille's revelation years later. She had destroyed Vito Russo's marriage, and the last she had heard, his life was in shambles and he drank heavily. Camille hadn't given him much thought over the years. She certainly hadn't felt any remorse. The way she saw things, he had got what he deserved. This Marie woman must have been related to Vito, and Camille wondered if Phoebe's kidnapping was his or Marie's doing. She did recall that Vito had a daughter from a prior relationship, although he hadn't discussed her very much with Camille or her mother.

"Why the fuck would he take Phoebe?" Johnny said, seeming to think aloud.

"Why the hell wouldn't he?" Camille said. "I basically ruined his life." Johnny knew the details of her Vito story.

"Yeah, but after all these years, why would he suddenly care now?"

"I don't know. He probably isn't thinking straight. He's an alcoholic."

Vito also happened to work for the Italian mob, and you didn't just go kill one of them, unless you wanted to end up dead, too.

There was only one person she felt might be able to help him, but she didn't know if Johnny would be on board with the idea. In fact, he'd probably hate it.

"We have to ask Billy," Camille said anyway, despite what was sure to be Johnny's resistance.

"Ask him what?" Johnny said, as though he knew what she meant but was pretending he didn't.

"You know, about Vito. He used to work with him. He knows him better than I do."

"You're gonna run to your ex-lover for help instead of your husband?" Johnny said, slamming his fist on the sofa.

Camille retreated from him. "Johnny, take it easy." She had gotten used to his temper over the years, but also knew he was under a lot of stress. "I go to you for help, always. You know that. But we need to get Phoebe back, safely, and I've been out of touch with Vito's whereabouts for years. Billy might know what's going on with him."

"Do you still have feelings for him?" Johnny demanded.

Camille shook her head, though the lie hurt to tell it. "No, Johnny. Think of Phoebe. We got to get her back home."

Johnny stared at her quietly and seemed to be considering whether he liked her answer. "You don't gotta tell me that. Phoebe's my flesh and blood, and I'd do anything to get her back, except sacrifice my wife."

"I'm not going anywhere," Camille told him. "I love you, not Billy." Which was true, although she still had feelings for the handsome gangster.

Johnny eyed her like he was considering what she said, and she waited for him to react.

"You really think it's the only way?" he asked, after a moment.

Camille nodded. "I do, Johnny. It's the only way, without involving the police."

Johnny nodded, and they left the house together in silence to get into his sports car.

"What do I tell my mother?" Camille thought out loud from the passenger seat.

"Let's just get Phoebe back," Johnny said, touching her hand. "Where's Billy living these days?" he asked after a second.

"He's got a girl. He lives with her," Camille replied, careful about her words.

"You seem to know a lot about him. You've been keeping tabs on him over the years?"

Camille knew that Johnny would dislike it if she told him the truth and answered yes, so she shrugged.

"Camille, baby, I asked you a question," Johnny replied.

"I've just heard things. Over the years, I've heard things. That's all there is to it."

Johnny started the car and didn't say anything. As they drove, Camille quietly gave him instructions from her seat.

"He better pray I don't come inside and beat his ass for stalking you," Johnny remarked after a while.

"It's not him, Johnny. Billy hasn't been outside our house; I'm sure of it."

Johnny murmured something unpleasant that she couldn't hear, and Camille was happy to ignore it.

Billy lived in a shitty neighborhood in the heart of the city, the kind of place the average person tried not to set foot in after dark. Johnny seemed reluctant to leave his nice car parked outside Billy's unlit building, but he also seemed reluctant to let Camille go inside alone.

"What's the name of his girlfriend?" he asked Camille as he handed her his gun. "Take this, and you can go inside." He knew from experience that she knew how to use the weapon.

"Her name's Pillow."

Johnny gave her a funny look then saw that she was serious and just shook his head.

"Hey, be careful," he said to Camille, grabbing her sleeve. "I'll wait here with the car running in case we gotta leave fast."

His words frightened her somewhat. What could happen that they would need to leave quickly?

Camille closed the car door, and with Johnny's gun hidden in her waistband, she ascended Billy's steps. The front door to the dark building wasn't locked so she walked straight inside. Camille touched the outline of the gun as she entered, as though to reassure herself she'd be protected if she needed it.

She didn't know which of the apartments was Billy's, so she'd just have to risk annoying the shit out of someone by banging on their door late at night. She started with the first apartment to her right, the first one she saw when she entered the barely lit hallway.

Camille knocked and waited for someone to answer. Then she heard a voice shout, "Do you know what time it is? Go away!"

"Hey, it's important," Camille said, having no patience for bullshit.

"Go the fuck away!" the voice, a woman, yelled.

"I'll leave if you tell me if a guy named Billy lives here. Is your name Pillow?" Camille replied.

"No and no. Now leave me alone!"

The woman sounded as if she hadn't bothered to rise from her sofa or bed.

Camille quietly left and went to the next door. At the rate this was going, it would take forever. Worry made Camille feel ill. She wasn't sure how much time Phoebe had.

Camille knocked lightly then could hear footsteps approaching the door. A pretty blonde woman around her height and age answered. The woman seemed calm, and not annoyed that she'd been disturbed at the late hour. She wasn't wearing bedclothes and smiled at Camille, who could see her teeth were a little discolored.

"I wasn't expecting anyone," she told Camille, very friendly considering the situation. "Who are you?"

"I'm Camille," Camille replied, offering her hand to shake.

"Camille O'Brien?"

"It's Camille Garcia now."

"Camille, I've heard a lot about you. I'm Pillow." She glanced at Camille's cane discreetly.

Pillow's hands were warm and soft, like the appearance of the woman herself.

"Is Billy home?" Camille asked.

"He always is. He hardly leaves the house except to score. I've tried stopping him, but he's a big guy, you know."

"I'm sorry to hear that," Camille replied, and her heart sank. She didn't dislike Pillow, but, personally, she would have done more than trying to stop Billy from scoring drugs. She would have tied him to a chair if needed.

"You really loved him," Pillow said.

Was it that obvious?

Camille didn't reply, and said, "My husband's waiting outside. I don't have much time."

"What's going on? It must be important for you to come all the way here."

"It's about my step-daughter. She's been kidnapped, and Billy might be able to help me find the people who took her." Camille didn't feel the need to explain anything more to Pillow, because she felt the woman already knew about Camille and Johnny's lifestyle from Billy.

"You better come in fast then," Pillow said, and hurried Camille inside her apartment.

26

U pon entering the apartment, Camille expected to find an utter wreck of a home, but evidently someone took care of the place. Pillow probably. Cigarette smoke caught in her throat as she approached the sofa where her former love sat smoking with the television on low and creating a glow in the otherwise dim room.

"Baby, who's there?" she heard Billy say to Pillow. She recognized his voice—low, warm—immediately. Just the sound of Billy's voice practically made her melt. She'd once been in love with every inch of him, including the way he talked.

"It's an old friend," Pillow told Billy.

"Who?" Billy looked up from the television and his eyes met Camille's. "What are you doing here?" he said, not sounding overjoyed to see her.

"Billy, it's been a long time," Camille said.

"I thought you forgot about me. Years have passed, and I haven't received a single word from you, not even a letter."

Camille tried to hide her shame as she replied, "I know, Billy. I'm sorry."

"You didn't give a shit about me so what are you doing here now?"

Billy was angry with her, and rightly so. She'd all but abandoned him when he became addicted and needed a friend.

"I got married, Billy; my life got complicated," she replied.

"Your husband didn't want you seeing me?"

It took a moment for Camille to nod, and then Pillow shut the door.

"Want some coffee?" she asked Camille. "Or something stronger?"

"Coffee would be great, thanks." She didn't realize how exhausted she was until then.

"Sit down," Pillow told Camille when Billy didn't offer her a seat.

Camille eyed the sofa where Billy sat, then settled on an uncomfortable-looking wooden chair at the other side of the room.

"You look good," she told Billy, after a moment. He did, with good looks, a little rough around the edges, a little gaunt in the face, with stubble and his hair disheveled. His body also looked a bit thinner.

"What did you expect me to look like? Terrible?" Billy asked with a chuckle.

"I wasn't sure. I've heard a lot of stories over the years."

"I'm not dead yet," Billy replied with sarcasm. Then he looked at her, closely, in a way that made her feel uncomfortable. "You haven't changed, Camille." He chuckled again, eyeing the gun on her waist. "But you've done well for yourself. I've heard you got a house in the suburbs now. Not bad for a one-time gang girl. Of course, I would imagine that Johnny's running the show now, am I right?"

His remark irked her a little, but it was true. After she became a wife, she'd surrendered to Johnny in a way.

"Pillow seems like a great girl," she told Billy, ignoring his remark.

"She is. She's not as good in bed as you were—you were fucking wild—but she's a good woman."

"Billy, stop it; that's disgusting," Camille shushed him, worried Pillow could overhear him in the kitchen.

"She doesn't care if I say things like that. She understands me," Billy replied casually.

Camille hadn't understood him sometimes, and she knew that.

"I'm surprised your husband let you come in here alone," he told her. "What if I'd been alone?"

"He knows you have a girlfriend."

Pillow returned with cups of coffee for each of them and set them down on the table in front of Camille. She handed Camille and Billy their cups, and Camille thanked her.

"What's going on, Camille? Why are you here?" Billy asked as he gulped his down.

Camille drank some coffee and found it very hot and didn't know how Billy could stand it, but he'd always been resistant to pain, from what she remembered.

"You must want something to come here after all these years," Billy said when she hesitated to answer him.

"She needs your help, Billy," Pillow told him.

"My help? What does she need my help for when she's got her husband?" Billy scoffed, and his words wounded Camille.

First, she had to get something out of the way. Because ever since Johnny had made the suggestion, she couldn't not think about it, despite believing it wasn't true. "This is going to sound crazy, Billy, but have you been driving by my house?" she asked him.

Billy gave her a look like she'd just slapped him. "I don't even know where you live, Camille. Now you're accusing me of stalking you?"

Even Pillow seemed put off by the suggestion. "What's going on?" she asked Camille.

"Did your husband put that idea in your head?" Billy asked.

Camille didn't want to tell him the truth and she believed him, so she said, "That's not why I'm here." She paused. "You remember how Johnny has a daughter from another woman? Well, after the girl's mother died, we got full custody."

Billy gave her a concerned look. "You couldn't have kids after your injury?" he asked delicately.

"Billy, I don't want to talk about this with you right now. The reason I came here is because someone's taken her. They've taken my daughter. Her name's Phoebe, and they took her right in front of me tonight."

Sensing her urgency, Billy seemed to become more alert. "Who were they? Another gang?"

"No, I don't think it's got to do with any kind of a turf war. At first, I thought it was Violet McCarthy."

"She's still around?"

Camille nodded. "And she's still causing me a headache."

"You know my opinion about her, and it hasn't changed."

Years ago, Billy had told her she should kill Violet, get rid of her, once and for all.

"I know how you feel, Billy. The thing is, it's not Violet who took her. It was Vito Russo's daughter."

"Vito? How the hell did you find that out?"

"We got this guy in the police department on our payroll," Camille explained.

"You're gonna ring the police?" Billy asked, using the remote to turn off the television volume. Then he faced her.

"No, Billy. I know you've been out of the scene for a while now, but you know, people like us, we don't ring the police.

You're the only one who can help me get her back. Vito trusts you; he always liked you. He'll listen to you."

"I haven't seen the guy for years. He probably doesn't remember me, and if he does, he must remember how I hate his fucking guts after you told me what he did to you."

"Billy, I got no one else to ask. I need your help."

"Is Johnny waiting outside?" Billy asked, with a slight sneer.

Camille nodded.

"Too afraid to face me man to man?"

"No, Billy, you know it isn't like that. He doesn't want to leave his car alone in this neighborhood."

"The neighborhood's a real fucking mess, isn't it?"

"I've seen worse."

"Of course you have." Billy smiled at her and seemed to be thinking.

"You should help her," Pillow interjected, and Billy quieted her.

"I can't help you, Camille," he said after a moment, looked away and turned up the television's volume.

She wasn't going to beg him, so she got up in frustration and headed for the door, thanking Pillow for the coffee. She turned to Billy on her way out. "Damn you, Billy. You used to have a fucking heart!"

"Camille, wait," Billy said, as she opened the door to leave.

Camille's heart raced with anticipation.

"I'll help you," he said. "But, first, I need to sober up."

"You're drunk?" Camille said with a smile. "I couldn't tell."

"I've become good at hiding it."

Pillow rose and looked at their empty cups. "I'll get us some more coffee."

"You think Vito's sent his daughter after you?" Billy asked Camille when she was alone.

"Either that, or she's acting on her own, but I doubt it. He drinks now, or so I heard."

"He's fucked up, like me," Billy said. "But Vito's not a good guy. I wouldn't be surprised if he convinced his daughter to take your Phoebe, to get back at you."

Pillow returned with their coffee, and Camille sat down again.

"What's your plan?" Billy asked Camille.

She shook her head.

"You don't have one? Johnny must have a plan."

"We're gonna go to Vito's place, make him hand her over to us." Then something horrifying occurred to her. "You don't think he's hurt her, do you? I wouldn't be able to live with myself if he did."

"I'm sure he hasn't, Camille," Billy said, and she sensed his words were spoken to calm her, and so she was unable to settle. "You're just gonna hope he listens to you? What if he won't comply?"

"He'll listen to you, Billy. You can make him listen." She paused. "You still have a gun?"

Billy nodded. "You think I'm gonna need one?" he asked.

Camille shrugged. "Maybe. Better bring it, just in case."

After many cups of coffee, Billy shut off the television, then got up and went into another room, returning with his gun. He signaled to Camille, then put on his leather jacket, which seemed to overwhelm his thin frame, and kissed Pillow goodbye. Camille rose and followed him. Billy tucked his gun into the small of his back as they walked outside.

"You know where Vito's living these days?" she asked him. Camille hadn't tracked Vito's whereabouts after his divorce from her mother.

"I think he's still living in the same place," Billy replied. "It's not too far from here, a little suburb outside the city."

Outside, Johnny had the car still running, and sat there quietly, waiting. Billy made a whistling sound as they approached the car.

"Looks like your man's done well for himself," he remarked to Camille. "Who would've thought you'd become a rich woman back when we were dating. It's a good thing you didn't marry me or else you'd have ended up poor."

"Don't say that, Billy. Money doesn't mean much to me anymore."

"Still, it's nice to have it," Billy replied.

Camille tapped on the car window, and Johnny reached over to open the door for her. He eyed Billy distrustfully.

"Billy's going to help us," Camille told Johnny through the window.

Johnny nodded at Billy, who, in turn, grunted at him in reply. That would have to do for now, Camille thought.

Billy got in the backseat, and Camille sat with Johnny at the front of the car. Billy provided instructions as Johnny drove them out of the city, over a quiet bridge, and into Vito's suburb.

"Do you know anything about Vito's daughter?" Camille asked Billy as Johnny drove.

"No, I don't even know her name," he replied.

"Her name's Marie. I pray our Phoebe is okay," Camille said.

Johnny glanced at her. He hadn't spoken much ever since Billy entered the car. "She's gonna be fine," he told Camille. "We're gonna make sure she's fine."

27

Billy instructed them to a small red-brick house on a corner street with a modest fenced-in yard in the crowded suburb. Johnny parked nearby so that Vito couldn't see them from his window and shut off the engine.

"You're sure this is where he lives?" he finally spoke to Billy.

"The last time I visited him, yeah."

"I don't think we can just knock on the door and demand they let us in," Camille remarked.

"I'll go first, see if it's him, and pretend I'm here for a visit. Then I signal to you from the doorway, and the two of you follow me inside. We'll pull our guns on them."

"Yeah, but Vito's gotta be armed," Camille said. "And he's gonna be on edge if he's got Phoebe in there with them."

"I won't give him a chance to react," Billy replied calmly.

After some more deliberating, Camille agreed to his plan, and Billy exited the car with his gun tactfully hidden. Camille watched from the car as he approached the house, opened the little front gate, then walked up the steps and knocked on the door.

"I gotta say," Johnny told Camille. "I don't like this plan."

"Then why didn't you say something before?" she asked, passing him his gun.

"Because I can't think of anything else we can do that doesn't involve blowing a hole through that fucker's door. I thought about doing that, you know, but it'd attract too much attention."

Camille knew he wasn't joking. But no matter the circumstances, they couldn't kill a member of the Italian mob without causing a lot of problems.

She watched as someone who looked like Vito, although older and heavier than she remembered him, opened the door and spoke to Billy.

Camille and Johnny prepared to exit the car, as Vito hugged Billy and welcomed him inside. They dashed out of the car and hurried to where Billy stood in the doorway with Vito at the other side. Billy removed his gun and pointed it at Vito, who unsuccessfully tried to draw his own weapon, but Billy wouldn't allow it. Camille and Johnny appeared from behind Billy, and Johnny aimed his gun at Vito. Then a woman, around Camille's age, stood behind Vito. Marie, Camille thought. And what did she have in her hand?

A gun pointed at them.

Camille tried to remain calm, but she couldn't control herself. "Where's my daughter, you fucking bitch?" she screamed at Marie over Billy's shoulder.

"Camille, what are you doing here?" Vito said to her with a slight sneer, and she wanted to punch him in the face.

"You fucking know why we're here, you fuck," Johnny said to him, in a surprisingly even tone.

Billy tried to force Vito to go inside the house, but Marie, a tall, pretty, dark-haired woman, kept waving her gun at him.

"I'll shoot you, you bastard," she told him.

"Where is she?" Camille yelled. "I want to see my daughter!"

"Shut up, you stupid bitch, or you're gonna wake up the whole fucking neighborhood," Vito said in a harsh whisper.

"Don't talk that way to my wife, you bastard!" Johnny shouted, lunging toward Vito.

Vito gestured at Camille's cane. "I heard you got injured. Now get the fuck away from my house."

She didn't feel like discussing her accident with this bastard, so she ignored him. "We're not going anywhere. I want to see my daughter. Now!" Camille told Vito and Marie. "I know you took her."

It was three against two, and Camille contemplated pushing her way inside, but Marie seemed willing to shoot. Then Phoebe's voice cried out, "Ma, help me!"

"Phoebe!" Camille and Johnny screamed at the same time.

"We're coming, baby," Johnny told the girl.

"Vito, let us come inside. Let's talk," Billy said. "None of us want things to escalate. This has already gone too far. Camille's daughter is innocent."

"But she isn't!" Marie said, glaring at Camille. "You and your bitch of a mother ruined my father's life! He started drinking, and he fucked some things up because of it. Then he got demoted, and it's all because of the two of you. And you've never shown any remorse, either of you. I've been watching you; you just go about your life like you're fucking invincible after the lies you told about my father."

"Vito knows what he did," Camille said, coolly, staring at her former step-father.

She'd never told anyone, not even her mother, or Johnny—though he was one of the few people she felt comfortable being vulnerable around—about how far it went. Not because she felt they wouldn't support her if she told them, but because she felt ashamed.

"You're the person who's been parked outside our house,"

she said to Marie. Then she looked at Vito again. "What are you planning to do to my Phoebe? The same that you did to me?" She sneered in disgust.

"You little bitch!" Vito yelled, jabbing his fat finger at her.

"Vito, let us in," Billy said, gesturing for the man to remain calm. "Let's talk."

"Daddy!" Phoebe screamed from inside.

"I'm coming, baby!" Johnny yelled.

Camille could feel him moving next to her, then the next few seconds were a blur, as he pushed his way forward, charging into the house, but Marie's gun went off first.

Johnny landed on the ground, between the front step and the doorway, bleeding from the chest.

Billy took the opportunity to tackle Marie and grab her gun. He stood there, pointing his gun at Marie and Vito.

"Don't you fucking move," he shouted at them.

Then he went inside the house and reappeared with Phoebe. Tears streamed down the girl's face, and her hands were tied, but otherwise she appeared unharmed. She screamed in horror when she saw Johnny on the ground, and Camille kneeling next to him, trying to stop the blood seeping from his chest and forming a vivid pool at his side.

Afterwards, Camille never could remember what happened next exactly. All she remembered was seeing Billy pick Johnny up from the ground and carry him to the car, as she and Phoebe followed him. Then Billy drove them all to the hospital.

28

Tommy knew he was fucked, that he would lose his job, as soon as Lieutenant Andrews exited the room Tommy had been waiting outside of during his hearing. The pale, furrowed look on his boss's face said it all.

"I'm sorry, Tommy," Andrews told him solemnly outside the room, as Tommy rose from his chair to speak with him. "They want you gone. I've told them I disagree, but they won't change their minds."

He was no longer a police officer and would never be one again. In a few moments, he saw his dream disappear.

"They won't reconsider?" he asked Andrews, trying not to sound desperate, although he was.

Andrews shook his head. "I tried telling them that you made a mistake, but were a good officer."

How his boss referred to his career in the past tense wasn't lost on Tommy.

Tommy didn't want to stand there and hear any more of it. What was the point? There was no going back.

He thanked Andrews. "Goodbye, sir."

Tommy loosened his necktie and exited the office building.

He could feel the Lieutenant watching him leave. The suit he'd worn to the hearing seemed to confine him and make him feel sweltering and uncomfortable. He still couldn't really believe what had just unfolded. He would never see his badge again, and that kept playing through his mind.

His hearing had been in the late morning, but the first place he went afterwards was the pub across the street. What would he do next if he wasn't a cop? He had rent and bills to pay so he had to start thinking fast.

A taxicab beeped at him as he crossed the street, even though he had the right of way, and his blood boiled. Why did people have to be such assholes?

As Tommy sat at the bar, drinking overpriced whiskey and eating the stale snacks they provided, he thought about his future. What would he do now that he'd never work in law enforcement again? His mother would probably offer him a job at her pub, but he couldn't imagine himself working alongside Sam every day.

His mother. She was all he had left now. Now that he'd lost his job and Dana. And if Tommy didn't do something about Sam, then Sam could send his mother to prison for a very long time, like had been done to Tommy's grandmother. The world was full of cheaters and liars, of those who betrayed you in the end. Tommy had tried to be a decent man, but it hadn't worked out for him in the long run. He, too, had been a betrayer. He had betrayed his legacy by becoming a cop. And what did he have to show for it now? Nothing. How had they rewarded him? By telling him to get lost. Tommy grasped his drink in his hand so tightly that he thought he felt the glass give. He knew what he had to do next. He couldn't let his mother be betrayed like he had been.

Getting Sam to the warehouse his mother owned in an isolated industrial area was easy. He simply called him up and told him he needed his help moving some stereo equipment that his mother needed from the warehouse to the pub. They arranged to meet at the warehouse later that night.

Tommy had parked in a secluded area outside the warehouse, and he waited in the shadows for Sam to arrive. He tensed when he saw Sam's car pull up, guided by the moonlight. He carried a crowbar in his hand, which he planned to use to hit Sam over the head with. Then he'd use the hacksaw he had inside the warehouse to dismember the body and put it in the old oil barrels that were inside the place.

He could see Sam's outline and heard him shut his car door. Then the sound of Sam approaching the warehouse, a place Tommy's soon-to-be victim was familiar with. Tommy felt a bit nervous and uncertain, and as he shifted, his foot moved a little gravel and made a noise.

"Hello?" Sam whispered in the dark. "Tommy?" Sam had always been a bit gullible, and lacked the street smarts that both Tommy and his mother had, and in the end, that had been what did him in.

Tommy ran out and smashed the shorter Sam in the back of the head with the crowbar. Sam cried out and tumbled to the ground, using his hands to shield his face. The first hit had been easy. Beating a man to death was a lot harder.

"No!" Sam screamed into the night, as Tommy stood over him with the blunt instrument, ready to smash his face in. "Tommy, why?"

"It's nothing personal, Sam. I can't let you send my mother to prison," Tommy replied. Could he complete the final act, the actual killing? Yet, nothing unpleasant raced through his mind. He didn't even consider he could get caught and sent to jail. Tommy had a lot of rage bottled up because of what had happened to him over the past few weeks. And the way he saw it, Sam was to his mother what Dana had been to him. A betrayer. To the McCarthy family that was the ultimate sin.

Tommy raised the crowbar high in the air and with all the force he had, came down on Sam's face again and again, smashing his mother's lover into an unrecognizable red pulp. Wincing as his eyeballs exploded from the pressure. Suddenly, it wasn't just Sam or Dana Tommy was angry with, but everything. His jobless future. His father's abandonment. That his life hasn't worked out the way he'd planned.

Sam made a choking sound and blood dribbled from his mouth, and Tommy stopped beating him, and took a step back, shocked at what he'd just done. He knew he didn't have the time to stand there contemplating, so he acted fast. He waited until Sam stilled. Then he checked his pulse, which he knew how to do from work. Seeing Sam was dead, he kicked open the warehouse door, and dragged Sam's body inside. A sweaty task, even for a big man like Tommy. He paused when he heard a sound in the distance, listened for a moment and then continued on when it dissipated. After the day he'd had, the last thing he needed was to get caught with a dead body.

Inside the warehouse, Tommy turned on the floodlight and shut the door. Then he took off all his clothes and set them aside. He didn't know how he would wash off afterwards, as the warehouse had no running water. But he'd think of something.

For a moment, Tommy stood with the hacksaw in his hand, thinking. Killing Sam had been surprisingly easy. Getting rid of the body... not so easy. He planned to dismember the corpse and put the pieces into two barrels, which he then would drag into a side room in the warehouse, which he could bolt securely. What he would do after that would come to him over time. But, for now, the body should be safely hidden inside the warehouse. The only thing he would have to worry about was the stench, but he planned to move the barrels before that happened.

Tommy put down a tarp then rolled the body onto it. He removed Sam's clothes, pocketed his car keys, and tossed the clothes aside. He knelt on the hard floor of the dirty warehouse and proceeded to remove Sam's head with the hacksaw. Blood spurted out of the man's neck as he cut, landing over Tommy's naked chest.

"Fuck," Tommy muttered, wiping at his chest, but merely smearing the blood over his skin, instead of cleaning it.

Eventually, he removed the head, and set it aside on the tarp. He dealt with the arms next, and struggled to cut through the bone properly but did after a few attempts.

When Sam's body was in pieces, neatly laid out on the tarp, Tommy rose and stretched his muscles, sore from all the hard work. He went to get the barrels and slid them into the room.

Through the room's sole window, he could see a light in the distance, very far away, and felt he must hurry. Quickly, he placed the body parts into the two barrels, then rolled up the tarp and shoved it into one of the barrels, shutting it closed. Moving the barrels into the side room took a lot of effort as they were considerably heavier. He grunted as he slid them across the floor, then once both were secured inside, he locked the room's door with the key his mother had given him.

The sobs gradually came afterwards. How had he gone from being a police officer who upheld the law, to this? But he did what he felt he had to do to protect his family, and there was nothing more important than family.

He glanced out the window where raindrops cascaded down the grimy, smudged glass, and didn't see anyone outside before turning off the floodlight.

Tommy opened the door and stepped outside into the cold rain, washing the blood off his body. He stood there for a moment, completely still, and then he fell to his knees on the uncomfortable, rocky ground, cleaning his hands as the rain pounded his skin.

Afterwards, he dressed his damp body in his clothes, moved Sam's car into the garage attached to the warehouse, then left. On his way home, he ventured into a neighborhood he knew well from his work as a policeman, the kind of neighborhood where it was easy to score drugs. He knew just the dealer, too.

The young man seemed surprised to see his face and brushed him off.

"I ain't stupid enough to sell to a cop," he sneered as Tommy rolled down his window.

"I'm not here as a cop; I'm here as a customer," Tommy replied, shoving a wad of money into the guy's hand.

"Get lost," he told him.

Tommy shook his head. "If you don't give me what I came for, then I'll call some guys I know in narcotics and tell them you're out here on the street corner tonight dealing."

Tommy needed something to take the edge off, fast and felt that the drink wouldn't cut it tonight. He needed something to make it all disappear for a while.

"You're fucking serious?" the guy replied.

Tommy nodded, and the guy passed him a small bag.

"You got a needle?" the dealer asked him.

Tommy shook his head.

"Here," the guy said, giving him one.

"How do I know it's clean?" Tommy asked him.

"You don't."

Desperate, Tommy took the needle then slowly drove off, heading to his apartment.

29

Camille stood outside Johnny's hospital room, watching him through the large window. Sheila waited at her side, touching her daughter's shoulder. Johnny had IVs and tubes connected to his body, but the doctors said he would live. Camille had refused to say who shot Johnny, and the hospital had to treat him regardless. A friend had driven to the hospital to take Phoebe home. Billy had stayed until Camille's mother arrived, and then they had parted ways with a promise to keep in touch. He had Pillow now, and Camille had seen firsthand the love they had for one another. Pillow was the right woman for Billy, and if she couldn't save him, then no one could.

"You should have told me about Phoebe," Sheila said to Camille.

"I knew we could handle it."

"And if you hadn't been able to?"

"Then we would've gone to you."

"That bastard," Sheila said of Vito. "I could strangle him with my bare hands."

"He got what he wanted—to scare me. I don't think he'll be back," Camille replied.

"Don't be so sure. Have you thought about what you're going do with the other situation?" Sheila knew about the issue with Violet's supplier. "You can't just wait for him to come around and hope he'll listen to you. What if he doesn't?"

"What would you do?" Camille asked her in exasperation at her mother's constant need to guide her.

"I've thought about it really hard over the past few days. Honestly? After all the shit she's caused you over the years, I'd have some of your guys get rid of the bitch. Once and for all. If she's gone, then her supplier won't have a choice, he'll have to work with you."

"Thanks, Ma."

When Sam Paul went missing for a few days, Dana sought out his whereabouts with urgency. She needed Sam's cooperation for her investigation. She couldn't demand answers from Violet McCarthy outright, so in desperation, she found herself drawn to Tommy's apartment. Tommy knew how much the investigation meant to her, and maybe he could provide her with answers. She knew Tommy had been fired and didn't know how he could react to her presence, but she had to try.

Dana parked outside Tommy's building and went inside. The hallway smelled of cooking. She paused before she knocked on Tommy's door. When she finally did knock, he didn't answer for a while, and she wondered if he was even home. Then she heard him coming to the door.

"Who is it?" Tommy asked through the door. He sounded groggy, which was strange considering it was the middle of the afternoon, and Tommy was an early riser.

"Tommy?" she said quietly. She felt she didn't need to say who she was, that he would recognize her voice.

"What do you want?" he said, rather sternly.

Her heart sank, but what had she expected him to do after what she'd done? Welcome her with open arms?

"Tommy, please open the door. I know you're angry, but I really need to ask you something. Please?" She used her feminine voice, knowing the effect it had on him.

Tommy let out a great sigh then opened the door. Dana stepped back at the sight of him. To put it mildly, he looked unwell. In fact, he looked terrible. Very tired and withdrawn.

"Did I wake you?" she asked.

Tommy shrugged. "What do you want, Dana? Have you come to gloat?" He gave her a slight sneer, and Dana winced, realizing how much she had hurt him. She could see his pain in his once beautiful eyes, eyes that she had once enjoyed staring into for hours. But which now seemed cold and hollow. Something in Tommy had changed, and Dana felt she must have been the cause of it.

"Tommy, your step-father is missing," she told him. "I mean, no one reported him missing, but I can't find him anywhere."

"He's not my step-father," Tommy replied coldly. Then he began to close the door, and she stopped him. The icy look in his once warm eyes chilled her.

"I'm sorry, Tommy. I'm sorry about what happened. If there's anything I can do for you, I'm here."

Tommy chuckled lightly. "You know what you can do for me, Dana? You can leave my family the fuck alone. In fact, why not blame Camille O'Brien for the whole damn thing?"

And Dana saw Tommy's true nature. His loyalty to his mother was clear, and he was very much his mother's son. She recoiled from his wrath.

"You know I can't do that, Tommy," she whispered.

Tommy stared at her in silence for a moment, looking at her

like he despised her. "I don't know anything about my mother's boyfriend," he said. "I wish you luck," he told her, as he shut the door.

Dana stood in front of the closed door, unable to move. She wanted to cry, even though she never cried in public. For she too had been in love with Tommy. And she had wanted to give him a second chance to do the moral thing. But now it was clear who Tommy had chosen, and it wasn't her.

Violet looked up from the bar at the sound of the door opening. She had just set up for the day without Sam. Violet had concluded what Tommy had done for her, but she tried not to think about it too much, because she had cared for Sam.

Tommy entered the pub, looking a little tired and more hardened, physically, as well as emotionally, and Violet imagined the act of killing had been difficult for him, as it had been for her the first time. It took some time getting used to, but once you did, you tended not to think about it too much afterwards.

Violet stepped out from the bar and greeted him in the empty room. She had good news to tell him.

"Tommy, thank you. I'm so proud of you. I always knew you'd continue the legacy," she told him as she embraced him. "My boy. You won't miss being a cop," she teased, but Tommy looked away from her.

Tommy didn't speak, so Violet kept talking. "Your grandmother's lawyer called me last night. He was able to get her sentenced reduced. She's coming home, Tommy. Grandma's coming home. We're going to throw her a big party."

"That's great," Tommy said, managing a smile.

Violet also had some other news to tell her son, but it could wait. She planned to keep her enemy close by, giving Camille a large cut of the heroin ring, to get her off her back. She'd come to the conclusion that the only way forward was to make a deal with Camille and Johnny.

Tommy pulled himself out of her grasp, and as his arm slid over hers, she noticed a new set of marks on his skin. She knew the sight well, because she had once been an addict herself. Violet quickly grabbed him.

"Tommy, no! Is that what I think it is?"

He refused to say.

Tommy ducked away from his mother's hand as she tried to slap some sense into him.

"Tommy! How long have you been using for?" she demanded to know.

He'd been about to answer her, and lie, when the door opened, and two tall, burly men, dressed all in black, wearing ski masks, rushed inside, carrying long guns.

"Shit, Tommy, get down!" Violet screamed.

The men raised the guns, and Tommy jumped in front of his mother, to shield her, but she pushed him out of the way, trying to save him and sacrifice herself. When they opened fire, a bullet went through her head. Violet collapsed to the floor, blood gushing from her forehead. Another one hit Tommy in the shoulder, forcing him to the ground near his dying mother. He knew she kept a gun behind the bar, but he couldn't get to it. Tommy crawled over to his mother, and put his hands on her face, desperate to stop the blood from pouring out. It was clear to him that Violet had been the intended victim, and he had just been in the way. He felt his mother's pulse, and found it faint.

Tommy heard the door opening and the men running outside.

He held his mother's body close to his chest as her breathing stilled, and she was gone. "I'll get them," he promised her. "I'll get them," he whispered.

THE END

A NOTE FROM THE PUBLISHER

Thank you for reading this book. If you enjoyed it please do consider leaving a review on Amazon to help others find it too.

We hate typos. All of our books have been rigorously edited and proofread, but sometimes mistakes do slip through. If you have spotted a typo, please do let us know and we can get it amended within hours.

info@bloodhoundbooks.com

ABOUT THE AUTHORS

Best-selling authors E.R. Fallon and KJ Fallon know well the gritty city streets of which they write and have understanding of the localized crime world.

Printed in Great Britain
by Amazon

82154184R00120